LUNA STATION
QUARTERLY

Issue 038 | June 2019

Editor-in-Chief

Jennifer Lyn Parsons

Editors

Rocky Breen • Linda Codega • Angelica Fyfe
Caroljean Gavin • Shel Graves • Cathrin Hagey
Sarah McGill • Cait Ryan • Carly Racklin • Shanna Ross
Tamara Lee Rutledge • Gô Shoemake • Margaret Stewart

LUNA STATION PRESS
NEW JERSEY

First Paperback Edition June 2019
ISBN: 978-1-949077-08-7

Luna Station Quarterly publishes short fiction on March 1st, June 1st,
September 1st, and December 1st. For more information and submission
guidelines, please visit our website at lunastationquarterly.com

For Luna Station Press

Creative Director - Tara Quinn Lindsey
Editor-in-Chief & Founder - Jennifer Lyn Parsons

LUNA STATION PRESS

www.lunastationpress.com

CONTENTS

Editorial

Jennifer Lyn Parsons

Jennifer Lyn Parsons is a writer, programmer, and maker. With influences ranging from Laura Ingalls Wilder to Jim Jarmusch, her tales feature a rare physicality with details that feel hand-carved. When not writing code or prose, she is also the editor-in-chief of the venerable Luna Station Quarterly. She finds joy in video games, comics books, discovering music new and old, and making things out of wool, paper, and wood.

There is a phenomenon that occurs as times change. When there is an overarching shift in the culture, politics, and science of the world, the literature of the time swiftly begins to absorb those changes. Science fiction in particular is famous for encompassing all that we fear as well as all we aspire to become and reflecting it like a mirror back at us.

H.G. Wells, and later Orson Wells's adaptation, played upon people's fears of foreign invasion. The B-rated monster movies of the 50s gave us mutated creatures born of our fear of nuclear testing. Sci-fi of the 1980's was hallmarked by corporate overlords and commercial totalitarianism. See Neuromancer, Max Headroom and Brazil for prime examples of 80's existential fears. Now we see Black Mirror and Westworld showing the dark face and fears underlying the too-rapid development of technologies we have little hope of understanding never mind controlling.

It should be no surprise then that dystopian and post-apocalyptic fiction is once more on the rise. We here at LSQ do our best to uphold the light and present a vision of hope and a respite from the darkness. Yet, even we are not immune to the times we live in.

Our collective fear of the loss of bodily autonomy plays out in the stories we present to you this issue. Climate change does not go unacknowledged by our authors either as more than one story tackles the aftermath of what now seems to be our inevitable planetary breakdown.

It is not all doom and gloom, though, so take heart. Within these stories, as with all great fiction of this kind, the heart and humanity we all have within us carries on.

There is triumph among the ruins, hope where there should be none, and a defiant thread of strength shared by the characters portrayed within these pages. "Hope without guarantees" as Professor Tolkien once said, is our bread and butter now. Hope in defiance of the darkness, hope in spite of everything crumbling around us. There is always hope and we'll be here keeping a candle burning so the light stays on a little longer.

L S Q | 038

Wired

Tianna Ebnet

Tianna Ebnet rose from the ashes in
the magical land of winter and road
construction, also known as Minnesota.
She is currently a MFA candidate at
Minnesota State University, Mankato,
where she works as a writing tutor and
freelance copy writer.

As a life-time and self-proclaimed
nerd, her passion is writing speculative
fiction, particularly stories with queer
protagonists. When she's not writing,
she is usually engaging with any medium
that has a good story be it books, movies,
podcasts, or games both video and
tabletop. You can find her talking about
any of those things on Twitter.

When people think of the Wired—although most don't—they imagine pain. It's a given really, letting someone cut into a person's head, hook them up to a machine? Of course there's going to be pain. But the truth is you don't remember any of this. You were out the entire time during the procedure, and you don't feel anything afterwards. Not the thin cables running under your skin and into the base of your skull, or the data stem you are suspended to. Not the warm air against your face. Not your arms or your legs. Nothing at all.

Sometimes you think of pain with a degree of fondness. The way it would throb up your foot after you stubbed a toe, reminding you that it was still there. You're not sure of that anymore. You'd been given assurances, naturally, before you signed on the dotted line. No harm would come to your body while you were Wired, you would be released at the end of your contract with a nice little nest egg to retire on. It would be like waking up from a dream. But they neglected to mention what kind of dream this would be, and it's not like there's anything you can do if promises are broken. Nobody's waiting for you outside.

In a way, it is better than Before. No more nights sleeping on the street with a knife tucked into your sock, no more giving blow jobs to strangers in exchange for a sandwich. Except you don't really sleep anymore. Sleep Mode is more akin to a doze, half of your awareness always engaged in making sure the air is being filtered and the lights are staying on, and while you expect that nutrients are coming to you somehow, you have no conscious awareness of waste coming in or out. But at least you're never bored. It can be exhilarating, being everywhere at once—so long as you don't think about how your influence ends at the door. You have the Internet at your metaphorical fingers twenty-four hours a day, hours of security footage, and an endless expanse of office emails to sift through. You're not technically supposed to read these, but it's a lot easier to hack the System when you are the System, and Security is more concerned with making sure you don't lock all the doors and fuck up the air filters than they are with personal privacy and who's sleeping with who.

You're not lacking in company, either. You're not the only Wired, not for a business this size. The sheer flow of information would burst all the blood cells in your brain. There are hundreds in the network and you can transmit back and forth. Some of them are lucid, friendly even, but most have been in so long they can only speak in error messages and binary code. You try not to think about getting that low. You keep your file on hand and skim through it often, just to remind yourself of what you looked like. Age:26. Occupation: N/A. Address: Homeless. Synchronicity levels: 85%. Prime candidate.

You look into that boy's eyes, staring sullenly at the cameras that would become an extension of yourself, and try to remember being him. It is getting harder all the time.

You feel the door to your enclosure open, the tingle of an electric card swipe, and it takes you a moment to narrow your focus and shift your brain to open your actual eyes—or what you hope are your eyes—that you so seldom get to use.

It's a Technician, and you can see in the way he tries to look everywhere but at you that he is new. That, and only the newbies pull the graveyard shift. Only the most vital systems are operating, so there isn't much to do except monitor your vitals and possibly clean your shit.

He is nervous, the way they all are initially. He is short, with brown curly hair that sticks up in cowlicks. Grey eyes, a mole behind his ear. You do a brief scan of personnel files, looking to match a name with a face. Ryan Morgan, age twenty-four with a degree in Bio-Programming. Young. Not only new to the Company, but new to the position. His hands shake as he goes through the standard protocols. For a moment, you are tempted to hold your breath so that the screens flash warning signals, just to scare him, but the momentary amusement is not worth the punishment that would certainly follow.

Eventually, his motions smooth out as he gets lost in the work. He begins to talk to himself as he types.

"Vitals look steady. Bit of a calcium deficiency. Definitely adjust the nutrient solution—"

It's pleasant, hearing a voice. A nice change from the constant hum of machinery. The last overnight Tech never spoke. Occasionally, he would grunt in lieu of words, eyes never leaving his screen, which chiefly featured buxom twins rolling around in a plastic swimming pool. You don't miss him.

Ryan, on the other hand, likes to keep up whole conversations with himself. Gentle admonishment whenever he makes a mistake, working out problems out loud, even punctuating his points with soft sweeps of his arms. Honestly, you don't know why he bothers. What does it matter if you're getting enough calcium or if your temperature is slightly elevated? You're still operating in peak efficiency.

He is about two hours in when he glances up and realizes that your eyes are open and that you are looking at him. You haven't been able to stop looking at him, actually. He's more animated than what you're used to. It is generally pretty quiet in Sub-Basement D, and something about his movements, the way he adjusts in his chair, wrinkles his nose when he's thinking, is endlessly fascinating to you. This is how a body moves.

Ryan's gaze darts away, but a moment later he glances back. You are still looking at him. He smiles, lips twitching without meeting his eyes. You don't try to smile back. You're too afraid that the muscles won't answer.

"Hello there," he says.

You stare, uncertain on how to respond. No one's ever talked to you before. All the information needed for maintenance is on the screen in heat signals, fluid output, and neural outlines. Your input is rarely necessary.

"I'm Ryan, the new Technician. I'll be helping to take care of you from now on."

Taking care of you. An interesting way to phrase his job description. In your experience, maintenance has little regard for your comfort. He's here to keep you numb, compliant, and efficient. If he's taking care of anything, it's the System. You can't fathom the depths of Ryan's naivete if he truly believes anything he is doing is for your benefit.

You feel a low rumble deep within, and with a start you realize you are laughing.

Ryan is even more surprised than you are. He leans forward over the screens, frantically typing, searching for whatever glitch made the noise.

This is not the time to test whether you still have vocal cords. You are both frightened enough. You send him a text.

Calm down. I'm fine.

He looks down at the screen. Then up at you. Back at the screen. You grow weary of waiting for his tiny brain to put it all together.

Who else could be talking to you? We're the only ones here.

"I—I didn't know you could talk," Ryan says.

Well, now you do.

He laughs, a short, nervous puff of air. There is a long moment of silence, but eventually he realizes that additional speech isn't forthcoming. He returns to work, although he still sneaks frequent glances at you, his shoulders tensing a little more every time he sees that you are still looking at him. You revel in his discomfort. Let him see the pinnacle of science, the flesh behind his way of life, and know that it speaks. That it has a name.

***

Ryan doesn't talk to you the next day. Or the day after. He tries to ignore you for the rest of the week. But he's very aware of your presence. You can tell in the way he fixes his eyes on the screen, gaze firmly forward. But his pupils don't dart around like they used to, and he doesn't talk to himself anymore, hypersensitive that someone is listening.

But he can't avoid the machine forever. Friday rolls around. End of the week. Last Friday of the month. Time for a routine diagnostic test. You dread these checks. First, you are injected with neuromuscular blockers to prevent you from seizing during the process, then each individual nerve ending is fired to make sure that they are properly connected. You feel a little prick before the numbness sets back in. Take that sensation and repeat it 95 billion times, while you are unable to move, unable to scream. It is the one time that pain isn't a vague, almost romantic concept. You are reminded that yes, somehow your body still exists, and in that moment, it doesn't seem worth it at all.

Ryan inputs the familiar protocols. His hands twitch. He is no idiot, he knows what this means. He makes the mistake of looking at you and fidgets in his chair.

"This may sting," he says, before pressing ENTER.

No shit.

The screens always go haywire while diagnostics run, your heart beating fast, breathing erratic and brain flaring with warning signals. It is the only time you are detached from the larger System, so that your distress doesn't interfere with anything important.

The lights begin to flicker. Looks like someone forgot to disconnect you from the secondary electrics. A prank, probably, hazing on the newbie. You would find it funny if it weren't for the quiet, paralyzed agony.

Ryan assumes the light show is indicative of a larger problem, but instead of scouring through the programs, he surprises you by getting out of his chair and rushing over. You are shocked to see his face so close to yours, and lancing through the pain is a soft pressure. A touch.

"Shh," he says, stroking your arm—you think it's your arm—in soft, circular motions. "Calm down. It's okay."

You want to light all his nerve endings on fire and ask him if he thinks it is "okay". But it's been so long since anyone's touched you. You can't feel him, not really. You're too drugged to feel the warmth and texture of his skin. But it's human, the first human thing you've experienced in nearly four years. It reminds you of Before, of fingers combing through your hair, the whisper of lips against your shoulder blade. You hate him for this. You don't ever want him to stop.

But stop he does. The diagnostics run their course, the pain fades, and the lights come back on-line. His hand falls back to his side.

"Are...are you all right?"

You're not used to questions but cooperating with your Technician is one of your main Directives. He is too far away from the screens, so you ping his tablet.

I am operating at maximum efficiency. Which is really all you can ask for.

Ryan stares at the message for several moments, frowning. "Yes... but that's an assessment of the System. The computer can tell me that. I want to know if *you* are all right."

You're...not sure how to answer that. Usually, maximum efficiency is enough. If the System is doing okay, then you must be doing okay.

I don't understand the question. What does he want from you? What's the right answer? You're not in pain anymore, but considering you're back on the standard numbing agents, that much should have been obvious.

Ryan purses his lips. "I just...I've never done this before. I do know the diagnostics procedure, obviously I know what it entails, but I never thought it would be...like that. The sheer physical strain, you know? Well, of course *you* know." He exhales a nervous, breathy laugh. "I guess...how do you feel?"

What does it matter? I'm back on-line and running smoothly. My feelings are irrelevant.

Ryan looks like he wants to say something else, but he lets the matter drop and doesn't speak to you for the rest of the night. In four hours, the next person shows up for shift change. She smiles at Ryan, taking in his rumpled clothing and mussed hair. Our time together has taken its toll.

"Rough night?" she asks.

Ryan shrugs, taking the coffee offered to him.

"First diagnostics check is always hard," she says. "Don't worry, it gets easier."

Ryan's shoulders hunch. He frowns, takes a deep swig of his coffee. "If you say so," he says, picking up his bag and heading to the door.

But he stops at the threshold, taking a glance back and holding your gaze. He smiles a little, giving an almost imperceptible wave.

And then the door closes behind him, leaving you in Silence.

***

You have been Wired for three years, eleven months, twelve days, and twenty-two hours. Keeping track is easy when your consciousness is directly connected to a clock, but it's not something you think about much. There's no real structure to your life save for scheduled protocols and Sleep Mode, so your perception of time is not determined by the hours of the day, but by the speed of information. It feels like you've been here only a moment. It feels like you've never been anywhere else.

Your contract isn't even halfway over yet.

The time is easier spent when Ryan is around. You watch him constantly, partially because his twitchy movements and muttering remains endlessly entertaining, but mostly because you know he finds the scrutiny unnerving. He's met your eyes more than once, beginning an extended staring contest. He always looks away first.

After about two weeks of this, Ryan shows up with a game of checkers. He holds it out in front of him with both hands, like he's offering food to a wild animal. "Fancy a game? These nights can get long without something to do."

After watching him for weeks, you have Ryan pegged as a True Believer. Someone not in this for the money or corporate advancement, but a genuine idealist who bought the Company's mission statement of creating a better world. But this? This is unexpected.

You want to play checkers? With me?

Ryan shrugs. "Sure. After all, you're the only one here."

You wonder if he's writing a book. Perhaps he wishes to study the Wired in their natural environment, test reactions to stimuli and so on. Or worse, he's a fetishist, and soon he'll be trying to lick the spaces where the cords meet skin. The Company typically tries to vet these people out, but there's always someone who slips through the cracks.

You consider all this, but the idea of a physical game with a physical opponent is too appealing to pass up. Ryan pulls his chair out to sit in front of your module, and you watch the flick of Ryan's fingers as he sets up the board. You ping your moves to his tablet, and he manipulates the pieces on your behalf.

You could lose your job for this. Or worse. The Wired are the backbone of the Company. Everything; all the data, the security systems, the very functionality of the building, runs through a network of Wired minds, which is why you're nearly always conscious. Tampering with you in even the smallest way is tantamount to sabotage. Already, you are erasing the chat logs, looping the security footage, but there's only so much you can do if someone tries to look closer.

"I'll just tell them I'm stimulating your synaptic pathways," Ryan says. He moves his piece to the edge of the board. "King me."

You triple jump his pieces in response, and he groans.

Why take the risk? Do you normally play board games with the office supplies?

"You're not a stapler."

But for the length of my contract, I'm Company property, the same as your tablet and the chair that you're sitting on. You move one of your pieces to the edge of the board.

"I know...but you're still a person."

And that's a revelation? Surely, you knew that going in.

"But you weren't supposed to be like—like this!" Ryan says, waving his hands in your direction. "You talk. You feel pain. You're sarcastic, for God's sake! I—I didn't know."

No, you didn't care. No one does as long as the lights stay on.

Ryan's silent, head down, staring at his shoes. "...I'm sorry."

This is a statement of fact, not an accusation. Now are you going to make a move or not?

He moves forward, leaving himself open for you to capture his last pieces. He resets the board, fingers tracing over the little circles of plastic. And you play. Again and again and again.

***

You don't really expect him back after that. You await the ping of the transfer request to somewhere safer. Less hands on. Perhaps Human Resources, since he cares about feelings so much. It's a shame, it was nice to talk to someone in real time, but Technicians come and go. You're not one to get attached.

But Ryan's back the next day with more board games tucked under his arm. In the next six months, the games become routine. Checkers intersperses with chess and elaborate games of hangman. You learn quite a bit about Ryan in this time. About his doctor parents, their disapproval when he decided to go into Bio-Engineering. Anecdotes from college and his time abroad studying the European Interface. His charity work outfitting underprivileged neighborhoods into the System. He also asks you questions, and eventually you start answering them. He starts small; favorite color, animals you like and so on. Small, impersonal data, easing you in before dropping the bomb.

"What's your name?" Ryan asks, drawing some open boils on your poor hanged man. At some point the game became less about guessing words and more about drawing the most grotesque stick figure possible. "All my supervisor gave me was a serial number. W-X6514790."

Catchy.

"Yeah, just rolls off the tongue." He grins. You like the way it makes his eyes crinkle, until they're practically slits set deep into his face. "What were you called before...all this?"

You don't want to tell him, not at first. You keep your name close. It's the one memory that doesn't hurt, and you're not sure if you want to share that. But you also want to hear him say it, to see his mouth move as he works the syllables.

You clear the screen, setting up a fresh noose for a new victim. *Let's see if you can guess it before hanging yourself.*

You don't make it easy for him. You limit the games and are merciless with his mistakes. You make him go on scavenger hunts for the letters. You draw it out for weeks, expecting him to forfeit and just look up the information.

"I don't want to get it from the computer," Ryan says. "I want to get it from you."

So, you give an inch, allow him a few more games, a few extra turns. Eventually the name reveals itself.

"Adrien," he says, and it's like hearing it for the first time.

You find yourself telling him more things, things that can't be found in your file, things you thought you'd forgotten. You lost your parents in the floods. Your earliest memory is of wandering the streets, alone and lost. Eventually, you get taken to a refugee center. A kind old man adopts you, lets you call him grandpa, and until you're thirteen, things are all right. Then he dies and it's back to the pavement, selling whatever you have in order to survive. When you were collected, when you signed yourself away, you told yourself it didn't matter. Your body hadn't belonged to you in a long time.

You were wrong.

Ryan listens to your story quietly, scrutinizing the chess board laid before him even though thoughts have strayed far beyond the game. "When I got my degree...we were told it was a choice. That these people chose to serve for the greater good. And so much good has come from the System. Clean, limitless energy, the ending of so much poverty and hunger. I thought it was worth it."

Maybe it is, you tell him. *Maybe it's all worth it. For them and for you. Not for me.*

"No," Ryan says. "Not for you."

You don't play any more chess that night.

***

He keeps bringing the games, but it's not the same. Ryan is distracted. Often, he will stop a game midway through, sometimes even mid-move.

"It's just work," he says when you ask what's wrong. "Things have gotten busier lately."

But you know he's hiding something from you. He is at the computer more than ever, his work so deeply encrypted that not even you can see what he is doing. Not without immediately alerting him to the intrusion, anyway, and you're too afraid of what will happen if you cross that line.

You worry that you've gone too far, destroyed this relationship with the truth. You just wanted him to know you, to know that there is a person within these wires and text updates. Sometimes, more often than you'd like to admit, you forget that yourself.

But instead, it seems he has gone the opposite direction. You frightened him with your humanity, so he is refocusing on the machine. He exposed you, dug out your past and emotions from the depths of the System, and now he's running away. You hate him. Coward, awful, cruel—*"Look at me, you bastard!"*

You said that out loud. Not text, your voice, croaky and garbled from disuse, but yours. Ryan probably didn't even understand your words but look up he does. He approaches you, puts his hand on your face. It comes back wet.

"Are you crying?" His hands cup both of your cheeks, his forehead leaning to rest against yours. "I'm sorry. I'm sorry. I'm so sorry." And then, he leans closer still, whispers into one of your audio sensors—your ears, they are your *ears*, "How would you like to get out of here?"

What? you text—you don't trust your newfound voice. *How—Is that even possible?*

"It is," Ryan says. "I've been looking into the Extraction Protocols. They're under heavy security so I've had to be careful. I didn't want to bring it up to you until I was sure I could do it."

Can you?

"It's risky," he admits. "It's not done very often. The subjects that make it to the end of their term are usually so far gone they don't have the capacity to leave. The shock alone could kill you. But I can do it, if that's what you want."

Is it? Deep down, you never imagined what it would be like to go back to the world. To go back to flesh and blood after years of nothing but wires.

But you'd be able to feel skin on skin again. Taste food on your tongue. Get out of this goddamn basement.

"Yes." Your voice comes out clearer with less syllables to deal with.

Ryan smiles, squeezes what you hope is your hand—oh God, you're finally going to have to face what's left of you. "All right."

***

You must be detached by degrees, a process that takes weeks. Every day, Ryan pulls you a little further out, partially so that your absence isn't noticed. The other Wired will automatically take up the slack as long as the influx of new information isn't too drastic. But it's also to acclimate yourself to living outside the System. Dependency is inevitable. It's like slowly introducing a fish into foreign waters. You have to relearn how to breathe.

Ryan promises that he'll take you away. He's been reading about communities deep in the Desert, far away from any sort of network. He brings you desert flowers, talks about the house you'll have, maybe even a dog—

"I mean, if you want that of course. We don't have to live together, we don't—"

"I'm no good with dogs. Can we have a cat?" you ask.

He smiles. "Yes. We can get a cat."

You think about Ryan, the house, and the cat to fill the holes the wires left. You don't want to miss the System, but you can't help but feel empty in its absence. A whole world, even one that strips at your body and mind, is a hard thing to let go of. And it's harder still, getting to know your body again. Feeling comes back first, and with it the bone deep ache the System was keeping you numb to. The data stem burns against your back, your skin throbs, and some part of you can't believe how limited a human body is now that you no longer have cameras to scan the corridors. Your legs cannot travel along electric pathways. They can't do anything at all. You feel trapped in your skin, muscles atrophied; limbs shriveled and tiny like a child's. You try not to wonder if this is just another prison of your own making.

"We'll fix that," Ryan says, rubbing his fingers gently over your temples as he heads towards the mesh of wires connecting your skull to the data stem. Theoretically, they should be able to come out, but you don't know how anyone can extract something so deeply embedded. "We'll have you walking in no time."

You don't believe him, not really.

"What if I can't do this?" you ask. "I don't know how to live in my body. Not anymore."

"We'll learn together," Ryan says. "I promise you're not alone."

You focus on Ryan's hands on your neck, how you can finally feel his heat, the dryness of his skin, and nod once.

Ryan tries to be gentle, but you feel every pull as the wires come out inch by inch. Once freed, you find there's nothing to support you. You crumble.

Ryan's arms are around you, supporting your entire weight with an ease that you would resent if you weren't so warm.

"I love you, Adrien," he whispers, and you smile.

You get to enjoy the moment for a minute. Maybe two. Then there are footsteps. Flashing lights. Ryan is shouting. He picks you up, cradling your useless sack of bones against his chest and tries to run, but he doesn't get far. There a soft thud of impact, and you are tumbling to the floor. A tranquilizer dart, you assume. You'll find out for sure when you watch the tapes later.

You wish you could move, could reach out and hold Ryan's hand. Let him lie to you one last time that it's all going to be okay. But the face that approaches isn't his. It isn't a face at all. It is a smooth expanse of plastic nothing. Hands grab at you, smooth latex, propping you up, finding a vein. A prick on your neck. You hear shouting. "Adrien! Adrien!"

It rings in your ears briefly. And then there is nothing.

***

They don't put you back on the drugs right away. They let you feel it for a while. Your humanity is a punishment. You scream even after they freeze your throat, your mouth opening and closing as you silently suffer.

You agonize over what went wrong. Was there a mistake in the dummy program that was supposed to serve as your substitute? Did another Wired or one of Ryan's outside contacts tip the Company off? Was it you? Have you been acting as the Company's eyes and ears, an unknowing pawn, this entire time?

Even worse, you don't know what happened to Ryan. No one else knows either. He is gone, all record erased. Ryan's fate is left to your imagination, the depths of which are limitless. Torture, imprisonment, death. The Company has no mercy for a thief.

You get angry. You tug against mental inhibitors that limit your access, trying to lash out, to burn it all. It would be suicide. It would be worth it. But security is too strong, you can't make a move. Anger turns to despair, and some part of you hates Ryan. He has broken you down in a way the System never could.

There is a message blinking in the corner of your consciousness. A text. Probably another System Update. The other Wired are steering clear of you. Nobody wants to be associated with the rogue element.

You try to ignore it, but it's followed by another message, and another. They'll keep coming until you answer, so with resignation you open the attachment. The words flood into your mind.

Adrien.

Your name and a little hangman sketch, waving at you from his noose.

You should've known he would be Wired. The Company knew better than to waste good material.

You move forward, into his interface. Your minds touch, merging and intertwining like electricity. It's not the same, you miss his fingers, his words, his mouth, but it's so much better than nothing at all.

Ryan is not taking his new life very well. Nothing prepares you for the System, even for those who consent, and whoever oversaw his intake did not do a thorough job. His shocked mind had reached out for anything familiar. He found you.

At first, his messages are fragmented. He doesn't know where he is or what happened. You have to acclimate him slowly, hold him as he grieves his family, his life. The only thing he has left is you, and some small, horrible part of you is happy.

You paint him pictures. Desert flowers, cats and dogs. A little house. He gets better, little by little, starts talking a little more, adding his own touches to the picture. Eventually, concrete forms fade into colors, a whole world of pixels, just for the two of you. You immerse yourselves into it, deeper and deeper.

Sometimes, thoughts flicker through the haze. You'll look at your partner and realize you don't remember the color of his eyes. What's his name? What's *your* name?

The question will haunt you, for a moment, but you feel the pressure of his mind against yours, the connection gentle as an embrace, and the thought will slip away, a drop in an endless stream of data.

The Zoo

Maria Zoccola

Maria Zoccola has two writing degrees and an enormous sweet tooth. She works in nonprofit, splits her time between Tennessee and Georgia, and remains deeply in love with the American South. She writes all manner of weird stuff.

At the end of the day, Ray, the keeper, lets himself into the loft above Wild Critters Snack Shack with a small silver key. It's a real key, a metal one, with sharp ridges and a little weight to it when it sits in Ray's pocket all day, secured to his beltloop with a retractable lanyard. A real key for a real lock—no breath analysis, no retina scanner, no thumbprint ID, no facial recognition, no molecular DNA readout. Old-fashioned security for an old-fashioned establishment. Nostalgia, or something in that neighborhood.

The Snack Shack slings old-world fair food all day long, four fryers going at once to schluck out as many deep-fried donuts and battered onion rings as Ray's hungry visitors can put away, and in the age of the peace treaties they can put away a lot. Folks spin out each day like they're making up for the days before it, trying to unearth the years of living they missed in the war and wedge them into every hour of the new dawn. The new dawn seems to require a lot of onion rings.

The smell of smoking oil follows Ray deep into the upstairs loft, where the last of the sunshine is filtering across the rows of screens and dials and switches and levers. The energy meter bolted to the wall above the central monitor is still safely in the yellow. Every month, the tracker pushes into the red as the days tick past, but under Ray's careful rationing, they've never once gone into the black.

And isn't the park worth the luxury, worth the monthly fight against the meter? The tall loft windows look out over the park, and sometimes at the close of the day Ray stands up here for hours, just watching. The visitors have all gone home with their onion rings and their gift shop novelty refrigerator magnets, and the park is empty but for Ray in the loft and the maintenance crew below, sweeping the paths. And the animals. Of course the animals, the jaguars and giraffes and the family of warthogs, the pythons in their glass case and the parrots in the aviary, the zebras and lions and three kinds of bears, the water buffalos, the armadillos, the gazelles. All the Wild Critters of the earth, spread out before Ray like a well-planned village, everyone arranged neatly by region of origin over the acres of the park, lit by the golden glow of evening.

As the sun sinks lower, the light sparks: from the waves of the park's lagoons, from the handrails and the metal fencing, from the informative plaques and the street signs. It sparks from the substance of the animals themselves, lancing through their glittering coats, through the thin transparency of their bodies. Ray approaches the windows and squints against the glare. It's like watching a recording from life before the war, something on tech so old it stutters and fails, the emerging film grainy and insubstantial, a memory, a dream. It's like watching ghosts.

Ray has been keeper so long his hands can work the controls by feel. His fingers find the master dial, the metal slick from use. One twist of the hand, one click to the left, and all at once, around the park, the animals fade with the dying sun.

***

The holograms are expensive, but it's all in the setup fees. Things hum along cheaply, now—Ray's even making money, enough to make payments towards his crushing buy-in debt. One eye on the energy meter and the zoo park nearly runs itself, a place for the old to bring the young, to point to the long-necked giraffes or the frenzy of the hyenas at feeding time and say, this is what it used to be. Before the war, before the peace. My small body, held in balance with an elephant. My fragile hands, meeting a chimpanzee's through the glass. My soft voice, roaring with a lion. This, here, now, is nearly the same. Nearly.

Nearly. Ray is plagued by the word. Nearly as exotic, nearly as fascinating, nearly as wild. His holographic animals can run and bark and jump and eat their holographic hay. Nearly the same as the real thing. Nearly! And what is it? What is the difference? Ray spent months stalking the park paths, glaring into first one pen, then another. The howler monkeys weren't loud enough. Fine, he upgraded the speakers. The tigers didn't drip when they emerged from their lagoons. Very well, he refined the visuals. The elephant seemed detached, unreal, a trick, curling her weightless trunk just right but not, in the end, striking at the heart of the matter, the essence of elephant-ness. Ray pumped in the hot smell of elephant shit and felt the weight of failure. And of course Ray keeps away from the elephant pen, when he can.

Nearly. Nearly the same.

***

When Ray was a boy, his mother brought him to the old zoo park daily as the war reached its zenith. His mother had a terrible fear of being trapped in their tenth-floor apartment if a bomb should fall from the sky. The open spaces were better, she said. Better for her nerves, at least, and better for young Ray, who jangled about the apartment if left to himself, tipping over boxes to hear the crash, jumping on beds, pressing his face to the windows,wishing for wings, for powerful jumping legs, for a body strong enough to break away and run forever, away from the warning sirens and scurrying people, and away from the way his mother's face looked when she watched the live coverage from the North Sea, the wobbly footage of the Cyrillic painted on the sides of drones.

The zoo was better only in that Ray could run himself ragged up and down the park paths, leaving his mother to take anxiety pills on the bench near the snow leopards. It was good for her to be beyond the four walls of the apartment, where Ray would watch her pace back and forth across the kitchen with a wooden spoon in one hand and her phone in the other, endlessly scrolling through updates from the war, dinner forgotten on the stove. Ray felt it himself at the zoo, the freedom of movement, the sense that all the world was a long road to run down. At home, they both spent a lot of time glancing at the locked apartment door.

Ray lost entire afternoons of his childhood watching animals. The brown bears wore a long furrow in the false rock of their pen pacing back and forth, eyes glassy, tongues out and panting. The chimpanzees screamed and beat their heads against the glass viewing windows. The tiger's cage still had bars, the sort that modern zoos had mostly abandoned because they made the visitors feel bad, and the lone tiger held within spent hours chewing at them, wearing deep bloody sores into the corners of his mouth. In the aviary, the cockatoos plucked out all their own feathers. Ray's fingers jittered over his own skin as he watched. He imagined the rip of it, a terrific bloody business, yank yank yank. He wished he had his own feathers to pull.

As the dogfighting from the Russian dugout in Scotland advanced towards the Eastern Seaboard, the schools closed and

Ray spent every day with his mother. They passed the frozen winter months at the zoo, the sky overhead a blue so clear it was like a drawing in a picture book, marred only by the contrails of fighter jets making for the Atlantic. The zoo did not close because the animals still needed to eat, and with the trade embargo in place and inflation stopgaps failing, admission fees were more important than ever.

In February of that year the city froze for so long and so hard that the elephant could not come out of her stall to walk her endless laps. Her feet rotted from the lack of movement and she had to be shot in the head. The zoo did it at night, and Ray did not hear the gunshot, but the next day he stared into a pen that was a different kind of empty than it had been the day before and thought he heard the echoes in the falling snow.

***

The dead elephant was a long time ago. There's no need for gunshots or their echoes in the holo zoo, nor is there a need for fallout shelters built next to the snake house or warning sirens mounted on the roof of the Snack Shack. Small boys still waste their energy racing up and down the park paths, but now their mothers post photos from their chip phones of the whole family smiling. The zoo has become a study spot for local college students, who park their tablet screens in the pavilions surrounding the peacock lawn. The war is something they cover in their history books, the trade embargo a lecture for econ theory. Ray reminds himself that this is a good thing.

It's the beginning of summer and the world is meeting the season with vigor, green and blue and warm in a way that Ray, a man with one eye always on the winter, finds a surprise. The park is full of visitors in sun hats and good spirits. The college students exchange their homework for picnic blankets spread on the lawn. They cackle with laughter when one of the peacocks walks through them, joyful with the way the birds' jeweled tails disappear into the mass of a living body and reappear on the other side. Even Ray finds himself lifting his face to the sun, and in the loft above the Snack Shack he fiddles with switches and dials until he's increased the animation of the animals to record levels. It will drain the energy rations, but the sunshine has put Ray in a mood for excess.

He walks the park himself to observe the results of his extravagance, marching up and down the long steep paths. He watches the brown bears splash in their stream, the tigers play-fight in the shade, the chimpanzees swing themselves around their network of ropes. He stays away from the elephant pen. All the animals are awake and energized, raising their snouts to sniff the breeze, and Ray watches them until the sun makes him sweaty and tired and he can no longer ignore the hollow weight in his chest. His face is frozen as he watches the hippopotamus surface from her pool, yawning hugely around the posts of her ivory. He examines this feeling in himself with a sense of frustration. He's just like the other old grandfathers, watching the wonders of his expensive holograms and wishing for the days when any man could trap a cougar in a cage and charge a dollar to see it snarl.

When Ray powers down the zoo for the night, the energy meter is pushed halfway into the red. With the rest of the month to go, Ray will need the animals at low animation, sleeping mostly, slowly walking the limits of their pens. He tries very hard to care one way or the other.

Ray thinks about his zoo all day and late into the night, sitting up in bed as a powerful thunderstorm rips open the sky. He watches the flashing at the edges of his drawn curtains, a light show that seems to go on and on. Thunder rolls overhead, loud and louder. He stops thinking of his zoo and thinks instead of the fighter jets of his youth, manned and unmanned, all of them shaking the air. What a time they had in those days, the whole city packing the dance clubs and the dive bars and the zoo park, everyone clutched together in a desperate need to bear witness to something alive.

The thunder overhead vibrates in the walls. But of course there are no more bombs to fear.

***

In the morning Ray fits his key to the loft above the Snack Shack and knows immediately that something is wrong. There is no gentle humming of machines, no blink of monitors. He turns the slick master dial to the right again and again, but nothing happens. Then he looks at the energy meter. The tiny orange arrow is pointing all the way into the black.

The city service tech Ray calls on his chip phone is sympathetic but unyielding. It was the storm, no doubt about it. Rations will be reset at the beginning of July, exceptions only for the hospitals, the fire stations, those establishments essential for life.

There are two weeks until July. Ray spends the day turning visitors away at the gates. Most are understanding. The mothers will take their young sons to other parks, ones with living squirrels that dart about with trembling whiskers, creeping so close that their tiny thrumming hearts stand out from their chests. It bothers Ray, the way his visitors' plans change so easily. Not once does someone say to him, "Where am I supposed to go?"

***

The zoo of Ray's youth finally closed when the city evacuated. When Ray saw them last, the animals were thin, prone to savaging each other in the night when the keepers went home. Ray remembers a leopard dragging her mangled hind leg, unable to climb her imitation tree. She paced behind the layers of steel mesh separating her from Ray, back and forth, back and forth, pulling the leg behind her. Ray hooked his fingers in the mesh links and watched her for two hours. He saw in her face that the walking was painful. The other leopard, the mangler, slept on a ledge high in the enclosure, pendulum tail hanging down. Neither acknowledged the other's existence.

The next morning Ray and his mother arrived at the zoo to find the gates shut tight. His mother's hand closed tight around Ray's, crushing his fingers. Slowly they turned around, back down the street, towards home. Riot police stood to attention in the mouths of the shops. An open truck filled with silent soldiers rumbled past. A jet screamed overhead. His mother led them back to their apartment with her head down. Late that night, his mother's phone began an emergency alert wail that no amount of button-pushing could silence. They packed, and left.

***

Without its holograms, Ray's zoo park is nothing but a collection of empty pens. Ray wanders the silent park paths for days, leaning over the railings, watching the grass grow tall and come out in patches of clover. The quiet hums through the park, through the cold Snack Shack fryers and the bare peacock lawn, pushing its way into the tangle of Ray's thoughts with a sort of soundless buzzing. He's nervy with it, moving restlessly from one pen to the next, watching dragonflies alight on the surface of ten different water features but not, of course, the one in the elephant pen. The path leading to the African Veld looms before him again and again, wide and untraveled, beckoning. There's a knot in his gut, as if he is waiting for something, some great event lurking around the corner, some marvelous catastrophe. The anticipation zings within him. In some ways, it is more than he has felt in his zoo in years.

At night Ray can't sleep; in the day he can't sit still. It is as if he is a boy again, that small boy who bounced around the apartment, who raced up and down the zoo paths, who wished with all his heart for wings. His fingers drum against his folded arms as he glares into an empty pen. June is drawing to a close, and in a few days the bare ground beyond the fence will be full of twelve small penguins and a holographic ice floe. He glances to his left, at the signpost marking the juncture of paths. This way to the lions, to the gazelles, to the elephant. Ray has the nonsensical feeling that he is running out of time.

***

On the final evening of June, Ray brings a small black energy drive to the control room above the Snack Shack. The drive plugs into the main console and the system lights up with a weak yellow glow. The drive is weak, meant to recharge a dying chip phone or tablet, not to power a hologram network. But Ray is only planning for a single animal. Tomorrow, he feels sure, will be too late.

He leans against the fence of the elephant pen in the light of the setting sun. The hologram inside dwarfs the young linden trees planted along the edge of the pen, a great African female, tusks as long as Ray's arm, gray sides rising like bellows with imaginary breath. Ray watches her loop her trunk around the middle of a holographic tree branch and lift it over her head, this immense warrior with her battering ram. The detailing on her hide is exact. The musky, rich smell pumped in from the hidden valves carries on the breeze. The speakers play her snorts and footfalls. It is nearly the same as the real thing. Nearly. Nearly the same. Ray grits his teeth in a sudden impotent fury. Nearly, nearly, nearly, nearly. Nearly the same! Ray imagines the elephant swinging her tree branch against the symbolic walls of her pen, imagines her knocking out a hole for herself, the crash it would make. He imagines her racing towards him, the great gray barque of her body bearing him down. In his vision, when the figure of the hologram with all of its trickery of photons and energy passes straight through the meat of his body, it is as if she is the one who is real and he the one with no more substance than a shimmer of heat.

Ray is struck then with the image of the elephant of his youth, from long before she went lame and was shot in the head. When it came time to leave the zoo at night, his mother could always find him at her pen. They would stand together for a moment, his hand in hers, watching the elephant sway back and forth. Her sallow head would swing like a pendulum, like dancing, like a long sad song was always playing in her mind. It occurs to Ray that he's never seen the holographic elephant do this. He is overwhelmed with a bone-deep exhaustion. He does not want to watch the holographic elephant any longer. Ray stumbles back a few paces to the bench in front of the pen and sits down heavily, closing his eyes as the tide of his childhood boils up around him. Oh, take him back! Let him go back to the old time, those days when the world knew how to dance, how to flutter every moment on the wingtip of disaster, how to dare an itchy trigger finger to go ahead and pull. That old song—it sounded like echoes of a gunshot in the February snow, a tune anyone could whistle. A melody everybody knew, back then, elephants and people too. It came in with the morning news and kept you two-stepping all day long. You heard it on the breeze, you drank it in the water, you ate your fill and asked for more.

For Ray, the new dawn has been nothing but a beat of silence that goes on and on and on.

**

Ray was very young at the start of the war, before the first shots were fired, before the half-hearted diplomacy dried up. The zoo struggled in those days to compete with the hundreds of attractions a lively city had to offer, playhouses and restaurants and weekend festivals. But Ray and his mother still came, because there were animal shows. Red and blue macaws sailed from fist to fist and kookaburras laughed on cue, and in the elephant pen the young female stood on her hind legs and took faltering steps across the bare earth. Her huge body was unstable in the air, not built for two legs, but when she came down the keepers would coax her back up. They held black rods tipped with shining silver hooks that bit into the muscle of her limbs. She squealed and shied away and up she went again, lifting her front legs out of reach. For a boy as small as Ray, it was glorious to see, a creature as big as a city bus rearing like a stallion in an old western movie. It was better than a movie. It was happening here, now, in front of him. Ray looked up at his mother, but she was not smiling. "It's all the same," she whispered, and Ray turned back to see a bright bloom of blood where the bullhook sank in too deep. One of the keepers hurried to douse the flow with a dark gray powder. A strange feeling started in Ray's chest, and his mother squeezed his hand so tight all of his fingers went numb.

**

The holo zoo falls silent, speakers shutting off with a click. Ray opens his eyes to find the pen empty, the energy drive gone dead. A true black night has fallen, and in the darkness, Ray understands what he has been missing.

The Extent

Johanna R Staples-Ager

Johanna Staples-Ager is a student
who writes speculative fiction, open-
water swims, practices primitive
survival skills, runs long distances,
plays the violin, studies biology,
and reads too much (and, at the
same time, never enough). Her
post-apocalyptic novel-in-progress,
Braving the New World, is based
on Shakespeare's The Tempest
and takes place on an ecologically
devastated Earth and an ark-
spaceship run by people who have
essentially deified Charles Darwin.
Her work can be found in the
Harvard-Radcliffe Science Fiction
Association's Fusion magazine.

Case 98020829, Exhibit 5.c: *Written in grease pencil on a series of "Preparing for the Henderson Scientific Aptitude Exam" and "Preparing for the Henderson World History Exam" flashcards, the following unusual manuscript was found in an abandoned house twenty miles into California Republic's uppermost ashfield, nearest Kinzie Township. The committee has concluded that inductee 2049458, Annika "Nik" Yang, 17, wrote it over the course of several days following her illegal break, accompanied by inductee 5243724, Virginia "Eden" Cartwright, 14, from Black Mile U18 Military Training Facility in Rust Knife, CA. Previous psychological profiles of Yang noted her tendency towards writing lists as a coping mechanism, as well as her distrust of authority (see Supplement A); however, staff had not detected that these tendencies had progressed to this degree. Re-working of Facility disciplinary, security, and induction policy has been enacted in response (see Incident Response Report 0078574). The corresponding flashcards are labeled with their original text in italics. Strike-throughs correspond to Yang's crossings-out of the text, and words circled by Yang are reproduced in bold. Further analysis can be found in Section 92.e.*

\<Transcript\>

SA179. *Q:* *What are the four fundamental interactions of physics?*

A: ~~The Weak Interaction, The Strong Interaction, Electromagnetism, Gravity~~

Hair: Sometimes our hair is like a pet we carry on our head. It's part of us—but it's not *really* part of us, in the way an arm or a leg is part of us. You can cut off your hair and walk around normal—completely unlike cutting off an arm or leg—but it can still hurt to be completely shorn, to have your head looking all egg-like. Hair keeps our heads warm—that's why it's there in the first place—but it seems like it serves some other purpose, too. No one knows this better than you, Smith. I always imagined you working your way up from the cadet level, until you were the one shearing teenagers bald, not the other way around—now I guess I'll never know if that's a lie. *Curly. Wavy. Straight.* You were so calm, as you gave me my first regulation buzz-cut, sitting in that dimly lit vestibule, telling me *it won't hurt, I promise*—you seemed to know exactly what was being taken away, like it had once been taken from you, too. I didn't think about that until later. When you took me from my old home, I was desperate for something, but I didn't know what, because I didn't know anything: I had just turned thirteen, my hair was falling out in clumps, and my body felt alien to me, growing unevenly, bleeding like I had been killed. We were all marked out there—we had scars like rivers, our ribs were raw shadows in our chests, a wonder that I was able to bleed at all. And you? Tall and unmarked, filling out your tailored uniform like a fairy woman, mouth full of words I didn't know yet, a pull to you like gravity, like the dents planets make in space. I thought you were a queen, come from another world; thought you'd take me to that parallel realm, like what happens to children in books. *Narnia. Fairyland. Pern.* Thought me and my small soul, me and my half-body, were about to be lifted, and hey—I wasn't quite wrong. When I walked into my first day of training, it didn't matter that the hair had once fallen from my head like dirty snow. I was bald, just like everyone else. You had made sure of that.

US209. *Q: Describe the most prevalent contributing factors to the fall of the American empire.*

A: ~~Corruption=the hacking of several major elections by....~~

~~Petroleum War=the drying-up of several major wellheads, leading to contested territory between Panoptix and Sublumin Multinational, causing bombing of....~~

~~Bombing of Wellheads=burning of the Texas petroleum patch, with the resulting chemical winter covering the Northern Hemisphere....~~

~~Solar Flares: disrupted what remained of long-range radio communication and electronic systems....~~

Scars: Scars are hurt and history written on the outside. Alright—on the inside, too. They're anything that has ever had trouble healing right, or doesn't look the way it used to. Scars are what you get to keep when your hair gets taken away, and they're for sure a part of you, like an arm or a leg is a part of you—you can get to be proud of them, like I'm proud of them. Or at least the ones on the outside. Ash-shrapnel on my cheeks. Ink-river on my forearm. Keloid where my finger was. The inside scars, though, sometimes you just have to plow through all that damaged tissue. Take them, Eden said to me, holding out her flashcards. They're horrible; it's all rote. I'd already filled up my own cards with crosshatched shorthand, making my lists smaller and smaller, until finally I'd run out. That was months before I met her—I'd been angling to steal someone else's, I wanted paper so bad. Still,

I was so surprised at her offering that I almost didn't take them at all. The cards were the first object, the first anything someone had offered me in years—so it was several seconds before I took them in my hands, said Thank you, several more before I told her you don't know how much this means. Eden for sure knows how much it means, now. She stays up with me when I write, did you know that? She doesn't want me to be alone. Eden's been reading my whole story from the beginning, even the parts that make us just fold in on each other, even those unreadable, unhealable parts. Back underground, her gift still raw in my hands, I looked through every horrible, rote, stilted question until I found ones that opened doors in my mind, and I could feel my story swelling up inside me, kicking against my skull like an unborn child. But still I didn't think I could write it. I thought things would make more sense out here, when I got out, if I got out—that ink-river scar's new, Smith. It cuts through the numbers on my right arm, my writing arm, and the ink has bled into the wound, and the whole mess looks like lightning, my veins, a river.

US039:   Q: ~~Describe the Marshall Plan of World War II.~~ At what point in the war did US officials know about the German concentration camps? What was the official reason for not releasing this information to the public?

A: ~~The Marshall Plan involved Allied aid to several impoverished European countries...~~

Tattoos: Tattoos are like scars, except you get to choose the story that's written on you. To an extent. You might not get to choose if the needle's clean, or the artist's any good, or if they carve a number on your arm, or the digits of that number when they do—but you do get to choose what they're supposed to be, the thing they represent. To an extent. Tattoos are less disfigurations, like scars are, and more symbols—and symbols are subjective; symbols can mean anything you want. Some people at Black Mile put tattoos over their scars, and other people put tattoos around them, like picture frames. Me, I just asked for a list of names—figured no one could mess that up. That's what most people chose, a list of names. Even though you told me my list was a price, Smith, one I would extract from the enemy, when the time came to go into combat, to sacrifice myself, to die—I've always turned my list of names into a form of remembrance. It was a prayer I could say to myself at night, a prayer that someday, somehow, I could still be lifted. Christopher Yang. Erica MacCrae. Marissa Yang. Emery Yang. See? Choice. The extent.

SA042: Q: *What factors contributed to* ~~Watson and Crick's~~ *Rosalind Franklin's discovery of the structure of DNA?*

Names: Names are like tattoos that go over your entire life. Choose a new name, and you choose a new life for yourself—in theory, of course. In reality, I think we keep our old names—only under our skin, like those dolls that open up to more dolls underneath. So when I chose my new name and did the clever, stupid thing in shortening my old one, I like to think that I kept the original: only deep down in my chest, like the smallest doll, the one that doesn't open anymore. Sometimes, when I'm just about to fall asleep, I can hear exactly how that name sounded—most of the time, though, it just hurts to crack open my chest that much. Annika Yang, that was the ghost name I bubbled into the answer sheet when I was aptitude-tested for military service, sitting in that abandoned high school gym, my folding chair placed right under the basketball hoop. A net hanging over my head, Smith, and still I didn't know this place was a trap. Eden's family was mad religious: she says naming herself for the promised land kept her holding onto them, their belief and their hope. Eden, because like all of us, she still wanted to be lifted. That's how I know Smith isn't your real name, Smith. We all want to be free of something. I think you used to be someone else, but you killed her—Maybe because you had to, but maybe because it was just easier, to not be a human being all the time. For years I wanted to be you, wanted you to like me, and sometimes I think your kindness, when you were kind, made me an even worse kind of monster. Because how can you live with that other body, rotting inside you? How can you live with the fact that you burned that smallest doll completely, until she was nothing but dead white ash?

US087: *Q: What societal changes resulted in the wake of the cotton gin?*

A: ~~Slavery, which before had little economic benefit...~~

Maps: Maps are what you make when you want to make sense of the world. They are at their heart, I think, vastly simplified versions of the world itself: when you map something, you're stripping it down to its roots, cutting out all the extra information, showing only what needs to be shown. So when I draw maps, and I draw lines and angles and circuitry, vents and ductwork, a thousand mazes, every impossible way out—I draw it all as simply as possible, and the world makes sense to me. You got over the fact that I make maps years ago, here, Smith. You made me prove the hard way, that I'd never use them to escape. My first maps were found in my boots, a supremely unoriginal place: there was no pretending they weren't mine. Enter Eden, who didn't know my open secret—Eden, a first-year with a higher score band than me, walking by the western wall with her hands curled within her coat sleeves, bald and bootless like all of us, when we were that new. Little bird, bundle of wiry muscle, brave of her to walk up to me: I've a meanness about me, like wolves or drill sergeants, hard and flint-eyed; I've been working on it for years. But she saw me drawing, this bootless new girl, and her eyes went wide and bottomless, and I knew, I just knew, what she was thinking, could see the thoughts crossing her eyes like clouds. Nimbus. Cirrus. Cumulus. "I make maps," I said, like it was the most obvious thing, and held up my left hand, so she could see my finger missing. But instead of saying "oh," or "I'm sorry," or "Let's escape together!" or charging uselessly to report me, Eden asked, "Could you teach me?" A need I'd rarely seen before in her eyes. I didn't quite know, then, that she was different, that she was like me, but I like to think I could tell. I like to think that we can recognize each other, us mapmakers, just from the places our minds go, when we've been left in the dark.

SA124: *Q: Name and describe the four forces of evolution.*

A: ~~Mutation, Gene Flow, Genetic Drift, Natural Selection~~

Escape: Escape is what you dream of when you can't live the way you do. We for sure couldn't live the way we did, and thus we dreamed of escape: we were children, the story goes, and you reduced us to animals. Or just convinced us we were animals in the first place. Reduced us to several thousand pairs of small and bloody hands. Not yet the blood of our enemies—mostly the blood was our own, as we clawed each other, as we fought, in dormitories and hallways and bathrooms, fought for the division of that all-important resource: your approval. Scars for days, we had: black eyes so black I couldn't see straight. Girls and boys would limp into history class—we were fodder, we didn't have to be healthy to make war, just violent. You spit-shined us to the sheen of fanaticism, and we shone like tiny, bloody suns: swum through pools with practice rifles on our backs, watched endless replays of the drone strikes, pushed the commands ourselves, when you made us; doled cruelty like we were born to it; rolled over, helplessly, at any action approaching love. And the days were numbered, for a near-escapee, a fiftieth percentiler like me—when indeed the days were numbered for all of us, when indeed we were to be killed in combat, if not exactly on our eighteenth birthdays, then not a whole lot after that. I realized we were killed only when we were no longer useful, too late—by the time when I was no longer useful. This place was a holding tank for the schemers, the wunderkinds like me—the ones most likely to lead any semblance of a rebellion in the network of factory towns holding this place steady. Rollingwood. Wirepatch. Broken Hill. Diamantina. The towns so many of us were stolen from. All that rote memorization was just to exhaust us, so we couldn't scheme straight—but so what? I needed your approval to live past eighteen; I needed the other children's approval just to day-to-day survive. Almost-escaping gave me less than nothing. I learned teeth and claws, after I was punished; you watched me. I learned that fuck-you-up look, learned to make them stay away from me—learned the hard way, bandaged my nine knuckles in the dark. Hid until my aggressors moved on to more vulnerable targets, lashing out when cornered, until one fine morning I was not-untouchable enough to approach one of the lower-profile packs and make myself useful. Paid my dues in fealty and obeisance, and if I was not valued, then, at least I was valuable. I had my prayers with me: my maps and lists and names and litanies, written on my flashcards. And I was alive, reformed, I had resigned myself: I was going to be like you, going to shoot for some high-profile home-base position. Even though most of me knew this was impossible. Then Eden came and blew that version of me apart. Newcomer, factory girl, scarred as any of us, scared as hell, but not one bit of her dead—even underground, at Black Mile, this place crushing us all under its dirty thumb. Even you. You only laid a hand on me once, Smith, and only when Black Mile decreed it; you were at least that kind. But you always had more of a choice than any of us. So no, I am not sorry for lying to you, butcher, when you asked me if I loved my country; I am not sorry, I am not sorry, I am not sorry at all.

SA067: *Q: What are primary examples of convergent evolution?*

Hands: Hands are such windows into people. Eyes can show you what they're feeling in the moment, sure—but hands can show you their entire life. Or at least the worst parts of their life; happiness didn't really leave a mark on us, as we met at the walls every day. I told Eden I'd actually lost which way was north when I was brought down here, and had chosen a direction that was arbitrary; I showed her how to flatten real objects, how to trace where the vents were, find their path through the walls. How to memorize this information, and destroy it afterward. She taught me how to scale vertical faces, in return, how to find the cracks where my weight could go. I was learning, too: Eden has the most messed-up hands of anyone I've ever seen. This is partly because Eden climbs everything—and I mean everything, she puts her fingers and toes in places you'd think fingers and toes could not ever, much less should ever go—and partly because she worked scavenge and demolition before she came here, leaving bits of abandoned buildings stuck all over her body. There are knobs of calluses and metal shavings the size of extra fingers on her palms; she has a smashed thumb, and a set of burns on her forearms, from leaching gold from motherboards with acid. Eden joked that the metal detectors always went off when she passed through, and held her pencil gingerly, because her hands couldn't feel very much, anymore, and said it hurt to clench her fists, because her scars would wrinkle up against each other, painfully. I was risking a lot, but blacking out the friction of the consequences: It seemed like if I trusted her, she'd trust me. Eden so clearly knew what it meant to be hurting. All her family's old-time religion back at her scavenge-factory, she told me, was really just a way to soak up their pain. When we shook on our unstable, tentative, impossible promise, even my own rough-cut palms, my own nine fingers, could feel how puckered and seamed hers were.

SA129: Q: *Describe genetic crossover.*

Stories: Stories are what you tell to get through the winter: Any winter, inside or out. They make new worlds, they make sense of old ones, and they'll keep you alive, if you want them to: Eden and I pretty much cracked each other open in those weeks, that way broken people do. Pretty much spilled our guts out. Pretty much told each other everything. So yes, I told her my real name, my secret name, and she told me hers, in return: We used these names sparingly, an endearment; our starved hearts singing, even as we crossed into barren territory. I told her how I made my first map, dreaming of the surface; how you put a knife in my hands, Smith, and made me cut my own finger off. Told how I did it, how much it hurt; the sheer amount of scar tissue sustained: hastily, like blue fire, how my mind went dark for a year. Told her how my blood spattered over my ill-fitting black mockery of a uniform, spattered all over your nice white dress uniform. too; how at least I had the satisfaction of that, of ruining something that wasn't mine. And I told her about my parents, who brushed my hair, told me stories, taught me the names of the stars. That big orange book they read to me and my sisters from, how it all just wrapped us in a blanket, made me dream while I was waking. Told her all the typical, massive losses sustained by people like us, the place their bodies are, bone meal in an ash field, the times I think of them, lying unguarded, in the dark. Christopher Yang. Erica MacCrae. Marissa Yang. Emery Yang. And the things Eden told me? Are hers. I can't write them down for you. But I can tell you that even though we had wrongness carved clean through us, even just the presence of another voice, another mind matched to our own, was enough, was more than enough—not to fix the damage, but to live with it. I wish you could learn from us, Smith; you are for sure a damaged thing, however upright and in control. We crossed whole rooms we hadn't touched in years, and those things you hide are never really gone, you know: they just lie there waiting for you to lift them, turn them in your scarred palms, hold them up to the light. I would catch Eden's eye during drill, force myself to pass her like a ghost, then feel the glow of our secret, ballooning inside my chest—people from my pack, my friends-of-necessity, asked why I was grinning like an idiot; they thought I had given up, by then, thought I'd finally crossed the line into that ash-crazed, self-denying, warmonger territory so many of us were pushed into. Meanwhile, half the sentences I wrote—scribbling on my new flashcards—began "Eden says" or "Eden thinks." I wasn't writing lists anymore, Smith, I was writing sentences. Compound, simple, imperative—the truth. But the best thing, the very best thing, was that Eden was absorbing just as many ideas from me as I did from her. Our minds sang with the heresy of it, and all this—all this within your system slowly eating us alive. We were making our own light, by the ventilation ducts; we knew with certainty, that we could not be subterranean creatures anymore.

US065   *Q: What factors contributed to Napoleon's retreat from Russia?*

Plans: Plans are really just prayers to the universe. I think they're necessary mostly in terms of persuading yourself to do stupid things: stupid things that might save your life, that is. Eden and I stayed up for three nights straight, shooting our plans down, finding everything that could go wrong. Most holes lay not in getting to the surface, but what we'd do when we got there: Down here had become our territory; it was difficult to think of mapping anywhere else. There was no logic to the stretch of the surrounding wilds, the way there was logic to ducts and vents and mazes—and I had skated along the unpredictable line of the rules for so long that breaking them felt unthinkable, unthinkable to go jeopardizing a steady half-life for the unsustainable promise of a full one. The strain of belonging and not belonging was cutting into me, surely as your knife had: I would trace my thumb over my forearm, my number, my list of lost people, trying to unlearn everything, everything you'd ever taught me about revenge. I am not sorry, I am not sorry, I am not...This didn't go on forever. A plan can't accomplish anything, if it's not implemented—and we found one, or it found us, and we followed it to the bitter end.

SA078: *Q: Describe the body's immune response to blood poisoning, in cellular detail.*

Blood: Most of the time blood's just swimming around us, all blue and passive. Some tropically warm river, no fish in it, just flowing along, marching soldier-rhythm to that unstoppable bu-bum bu-bum bu-bum. But when it gets outside our bodies—well. What a mess. No wonder I, thirteen, had found my new, bleeding body so uncomfortable. On that day, that fateful day, Eden and I were some hundred yards closer to the surface, and it was three in the morning—razors, could not have been more on edge than us. Even Eden, scaler of everything, had her hands shaking. The maps were shaking, too, impossibly bright in my head, and I believed in them almost entirely because I had to, because at that point, I had no choice. We had to cut from the lower maintenance tunnels into the upper ones, and I was leading us up a vertical exhaust shaft, after Eden had led us up the last one: She was on the walkway below me, the rope tight around my waist, and I reached my hand up, towards the vein-thin horizontal duct I knew would be there, back braced against the opposite wall. My mind had already cast itself into the upper tunnels, their laddered expanse, where the going would be easy—I was that jittery kind of confident, living half in the world where we'd already escaped, half in this one. But my foot slipped, and I cast out my extended arm for balance, and ended up levering full force on a set of exposed screws, calling out, the soft part of my forearm impaled. A. B. Negative. There was a clock in my body, ticking down to nothing. I should've braced myself, should've something, but my head was not where I left it, my legs were failing, I could feel the screws rip into me as I fell—and then nothing, for a long time, nothing, as if I had ceased to exist. (Section continues on card SA056 Q: In which part of the brain is vested control of the rhythm of the heart and lungs?) I woke dimly aware of an ache, and the fact that something was missing—but the crazy patterns our lights made, the shine and wobble of hundreds of feet of metal pulsed against my skull, making it difficult to cultivate awareness of anything else. I thought, stupidly, wow, this is what it must be like to be in shock. Then what was missing came back to me. It was pain, and I nearly blacked out again, it was so bad: vomited, half-curled, into my own lap, then fell onto my back again, onto the walkway below the duct, bruised everywhere, elbow broken where I'd tried to roll; this tightness over my forearms, someone crying, unable to speak. It was Eden, crying, or at least I thought it was—the sound seemed to come from everywhere. Please, she was saying, please, Annika, please, please...Poor dear, I thought distantly, She's lost the map. And then, I am the map. I am the goddamn map, I am, I am, I am, and I opened my mouth, and sound came out, up three hundred feet to a maintenance ladder breach the fire door avoid the alarm three flights of ladder-stairs and a shaft turn right turn left and my voice was the voice of a harpy, clawing her way out of hell. Eden had bound my arm with her shirt, I learned later—her uniform shirt, the shirt you gave her, saving my life. We were on our feet by then, and I was not part of this world anymore, was half-walking, half-stumbling, every step tearing something out of me, towed up rope-lengths into the hot dull roar of the exhaust ducts, coughed out of the lungs of that massive animal—blood on my hands, blood on Eden's hands, Eden breathing short breaths, saying come on, come on, you're strong, you can do this, we'll make it, we can't not make it, and the sheer amount I loved her, was not containable, by then. Dripping onto our chests, smeared on the rungs of ladders thousands of feet below the Earth, tracing up towards the surface, the sickest map imaginable: the biggest mess I've ever made; mine, mine, mine.

SA096. Q: *Describe Solar Flares.*

The Sun is bigger than anything we can imagine. It could swallow a million Earths, and still come up hungry: the layers of it are gargantuan, made of matter so hot it glows; matter so hot it isn't even matter anymore. I don't think people have the vocabulary for something that big, that bright-lit, floating in the middle of nothing. When we reached the surface, Eden and I, the sun had come up, and I saw only the barest sherbet smear of it before I passed out. Wordless. You were waking up then, Smith, at the same time we all woke up, down there. Reveille blared into your ears through the speakers. Someone had noticed the ropes in the gymnasium were missing—did they tell you? Did you know it was me? The tunnel lights ran full-brightness, as you and the others put on your uniforms, whipped bodies to motion, spit on the students' shoes that were not shined enough—meanwhile I, Annika, desperate mapmaker, wordless, because I had not seen that sun in four years. The sun destroyed all the radio communications in my town, Smith, four years ago. We had no way of knowing the bombs were coming. You came in like an angel, and left everyone but me to die. Eden's told me about the Biblical apocalypse, so I know: The fire this time. It sounds ridiculous, because it's true. But here, here: the sun will come up tomorrow, and the next day, and the next. The sun will rise in the east and set in the west; and I will know which way north is, simply by where my shadow falls.

US190:   **Q:**   *What factors contributed to the American Revolution?*

Hair: Hair definitely serves some other purpose, definitely. I know this better than you, Smith, because I had forgotten it. My hair was flopping into my eyes—Could I even remember what texture it was? Could I remember the braids my mother put it in?—and Eden's was crinkling and waving above her head; we had forgotten what it was like, to be that kind of whole, to have that kind of choice about our bodies. In the end we cut each other's hair with a sharpened piece of glass, near a frigid river; figured it would be best, so the filters we stole would fit right. We cried, doing this. We folded our bodies close to each other and we cried. We hadn't realized it would hurt that much, to try to be human beings again. My broken elbow was tender, healing well enough, though it hurt all the time; my forearm kept clean, we hoped, forming this jagged river of a scar—that scar tearing right through my number, Smith, jagged like veins, lightning, a lit speck of ash. We were still running-rabbit creatures—seven, preferably eight steps ahead of you and your sensors and rifles, we were; soaked in river mud to hide our scent, sleeping in houses half-collapsed, we were; waking early, hands glued on our stolen chain-stripped bicycles, destroying all of the evidence, sleeping exhausted, we were, the sleep of the just and the dead. Still, at night, our plan, its final, glorious steps, was so close we could taste it. Even you with your white uniform, your unrationed meals can't know the pleasure of that. We are selfish, a contained unit, whatever heresy we wish dancing on our tongues, because the final day, the day of our vanishment, is almost-almost-almost at hand—and I've spent time, so much time, working on this. I needed to hammer the truth out, even if it never will fit quite right. Needed to tell you that truth, even if you'd never hear it. I am my own kind of beautiful choice-making monster, Smith, one with nothing to do with you. And Eden's asleep, now, and she is beautiful: Her hair is jagged where I cut it with the glass knife, my own head bears similar asymmetries, and her eyes are closed, forehead scrunched, in that tiny furrow that's always there when she dreams. We are not well-fed, here, but we are alive, living, without a question or a doubt—and I am sorry, I am sorry for you. You who made us sleep on metal beds with the springs sticking out. You who took our names and gave us nothing in exchange. You asked us to erase ourselves, and here we are: gone.

<End transcript>

Update: *Further disciplinary action was taken following the illegal release of Exhibit 5.c by a student within the Black Mile community. Re-working of Facility policy has been enacted in response. Officer Angela Smith has requested indefinite leave; the request has not been granted. (See Request Response Form 90875857.) The search for Yang and Cartwright continues up the coast. Further evidence has not been found.*

Looking For Sentience

Mary E. Lowd

Mary E. Lowd is a science-fiction
and furry writer in Oregon. More
than 130 of her short stories have
been published. Her novels include
the Otters In Space trilogy, In a
Dog's World, and The Snake's
Song: A Labyrinth of Souls Novel
Her fiction has won an Ursa Major
Award and two Cóyotl Awards.

Light glinted off the tips of the spires that rose from the rocky asteroid base of Kau Meti as Gerangelo's shuttle approached. The yellow sunlight caught the metal of the spires in just the right way to gleam enticingly, like a wink and the promise of a shiny, exciting future. Gerangelo was not impressed. He was familiar with the promises humans made to themselves and others—with words, with shiny buildings, even with contracts filled with legally binding language. They made promises and broke them. Sometimes, though, when they wouldn't break their own promises, Gerangelo had to break their promises for them—fight his way through with a machete of righteousness.

Gerangelo parked his shuttle on one of the asteroid's landing pads. As soon as the shuttle's engines powered down, the pad descended beneath the asteroid's surface into the hollowed out center. It was like a parking garage inside an asteroid. Gerangelo left his shuttle in the care of one of the Heffen attendants: a canid woman wearing a jumpsuit uniform over her thick red fur. The uniform was emblazoned with the words GENE-TECH.

Gerangelo took an elevator up into one of the spires. He may have been a robot, but he looked like an extremely handsome human man—dark hair, dark eyes, chiseled nose, and broad shoulders. His creator had designed him that way—as her perfect man. But, he'd outgrown her, taken the sentience tests, and then sued her for half of her Robot Emporium.

Gerangelo had become a roboticist in his own right. In his spare time, he helped educate other sentient robots about their rights. Sure, there were plenty of sub-sentient deck-scrubbers roaming around Crossroads Station, keeping the station clean and possessing the intellect of a counting program (or, a goldfish, in organic-speak.) But, there were also sentient robots, designed for more complicated tasks, who had never been informed by their creators or purchasers that sentient creatures—organic OR robotic—could not be enslaved: legally, morally, ethically, or at all.

Since Gerangelo looked like a human—and a handsome, well-dressed one at that—he was greeted on the other side of the elevator by enthusiastic sales reps. The human woman and Heffen man weren't wearing jumpsuits like the parking attendant, but their crisp business suits were also emblazoned with the all caps word GENE-TECH.

"Welcome to Gene-Tech," the human said. Her hair was about the same shade of red as the Heffen man's fur. "I'm Laura Edel, and this is Jeffa Kour. We're happy to give you a tour of our facilities and talk to you about your needs and what our scientists are capable of."

"I've heard good things," Gerangelo said dryly. He'd actually heard horrible things. Mostly one thing—a plea for help. Somewhere in this institution, a sentient robot was being enslaved and had managed to sneak a message to Gerangelo's shop, Robots 4 Robots, on Crossroads Station. A deeply stirring, heartfelt plea. At least, it would have been, if robots were inflicted with hearts.

Gerangelo intended to find the robot, help them, and see to it that they had the knowledge and tools needed to free themselves from their human-made captivity. "I'd love to start with a tour." Gerangelo flashed a smile that he knew made human women go all melty inside. His eyes sparkled at Laura, and he knew it. Then, he nodded at Jeffa, and the Heffen nodded back.

"Right this way," Jeffa said, gesturing with a paw fringed by long orange fur that overflowed the tight cuff of his shirt sleeve.

Gerangelo followed the human and Heffen through the halls and stairs and laboratories of the high rise building, tuning out their patter about gengineering and custom-designed organics. From the outside, this building had looked like a futuristic metal spire. On the inside it was just an office building. But, the windows did all look out on the gleaming semi-circle of the asteroid belt and a field of stars behind it. Without an atmosphere refracting the sunlight, the yellow sun—dimmed by photoreactive glass—and the distant stars shared the heavens. The view was nice.

Gerangelo tried to stay focused, watching for robots who had the potential for more than they were currently doing. None of the cleaning robots—which looked like trash cans on wheels—were made from high enough quality materials to imply their brains had the kind of expensive circuitry necessary to support sentience in such small housings.

For a computer to be capable of sentience, it had to be large enough, or the circuitry had to be small enough, to allow the processor to pass a critical threshold in terms of operations per second. The exact number had not been quantified. Gerangelo had pushed for that ambiguity when he'd joined the board in charge of the sentience tests. He didn't want to rule out the possibility of what he called Slow Sentience. Thinking can happen at all speeds. The question isn't: is it fast? The question is: is it self aware?

Nonetheless, there were trends. And Gerangelo couldn't tilt after every mechanical windmill. He didn't have time. So, he ignored the cleaning robots. He wondered if the sentient robot here could be the building itself. If the computers were networked, then he might not be looking for a robot so much as a sentient computer system. There were a lot of computers here.

"So far, we've only showed you the work rooms where ideas are developed," the Heffen man woofed. "Shall we show you the exciting part now?"

"The gallery, if you will?" the human added. She smiled like she was trying to flirt with Gerangelo.

Belatedly, he remembered that he'd been encouraging her to think they were flirting, in order to keep her cooperative. So, he smiled back and said, "Please do!" She wouldn't have noticed the slight delay. Human brains didn't move fast enough to keep up with him.

The human and Heffen showed Gerangelo into a penthouse atrium—the very top of their particular spire. Stars shone through all the slanted windows above, slightly obscured by the tangled green reflections of the trees and shrubbery filling the large room. Birds squawked and frogs croaked. He heard the violin-like chirping of insects. It was a cacophony of organic noise.

"Well, isn't that lovely," Gerangelo said, trying to hide his distaste.

"Everything in here has been genetically tweaked for a specific purpose," the human said, reaching down to pick up one of the frogs. It gleamed wetly on her hand like an emerald. Except squishy and blobby, filled with blood and organs. Total ick.

Really, nothing like an emerald. "This amphibious chimera was designed using DNA from a variety of frog-like creatures from different star systems, primarily the Emeraldback Flummox Frog from Orion's Boot Toe."

If androids had a gag reflex, Gerangelo would have gagged. "Gorgeous," he forced himself to say. Maybe there was a caretaker robot somewhere in this mess of photosynthetic organisms feeding the animals and tending the plants—a job complicated enough that it might lead a robot to develop sentience. He didn't see any silver gleams among the green though. It was all squishy green stuff in here, except for the occasional ostentatiously colored macaw or butterfly.

"Don't you want to know what the frog was designed to do?" the Heffen woofed.

Uh oh, they were noticing that he didn't care about their designer organics. "Right, yes," Gerangelo said. "I was simply distracted—" He gestured about at all of the awful organics. "—by all the...amazing...things in here."

Laura beamed. She held the frog toward him. "Would you like to hold it?" The frog opened its wide mouth and started singing a syncopated croaking beat. "Its skin exudes a chemical that humans—like us—find soothing, and receptors in its toes pick up the emotions of the person holding it and translate them into song."

"It's a mood frog!" the Heffen woofed.

"That is so very delightful," Gerangelo said, backing away. "But there's so much in here...It's a little overwhelming. Do you mind if I look around by myself for a while?"

The human and Heffen sales reps exchanged a glance, and the

Heffen shrugged. The human looked a little hurt that Gerangelo didn't want to keep flirting with her. But she said, "sure, we'll be right over here if you have any questions."

The Heffen added, "and for when you're ready to start talking about your own project, we can give you lots of information about options and pricing."

Gerangelo took off into the rainforest of designer trees. There had to be a robot somewhere in here. Interacting with organics was notoriously difficult work—organics could be so finicky and erratic. They required a delicate touch and keen intelligence, exactly the ingredients that often led to a robot developing sentience. It was a sad irony: working with organics led robots to develop the kind of intelligence that made them *not want to work with organics.*

Gerangelo stumbled through the forest, tripping over tree roots and wishing he were back on the smooth metal floors of Crossroads Station. He aimed for the far side of the atrium; perhaps there was a computer bank with atmospheric controls hiding over there? That could be a complex enough process to lead to the development of sentience.

Gerangelo did find a computer bank, and he poked at it briefly, typing a few test commands into the console. Of course, it was password locked, but he had a knack for hacking and finding backdoors into programs. If there was a self-aware intelligence hiding in the computer's software, it would want to reach out to him. After all, someone had summoned him here, asking for help.

"Ehks-scoooze may," a rough voice spoke from behind.

Gerangelo turned around to see a fuzzy brown creature, about half his height, with a long muzzle and round ears, staring at him from soulful eyes. It looked a bit like a wolverine or badger, except it was standing on hind legs, shoulders slumped forward but still, bipedal.

"I'm not one of the workers here," Gerangelo said. He gestured vaguely back the way he'd come. "There are some of your people over there. If you're...hungry...or whatever, go bother them." Organics were always getting hungry.

"Aihr yooo Geh-ran-geh-low?" the badger creature spoke each syllable carefully; the Solanese language did not fit the shape of its muzzle well.

"Yeees..." Gerangelo recoiled from the gengineered monstrosity. He could see where this was going, and he didn't like it. Organics were bad enough, but now humans were gengineering quasi-sentient organics? Weren't they satisfied by all of the alien races they'd met out here in the stars? Naturally evolved organic sentients like the canine Heffens abounded on the Goldilocks planets in the galaxy. Human scientists didn't need to try to create more.

Gerangelo already had his hands full defending all of the fully sentient robots that humans tried to enslave, and now he had quasi-sentient organics reaching out to him as well. Robots were his work; organics should, *at least*, take care of their own kind.

"Cawl-ed yooo for halp," the badger said.

"I work with robots," Gerangelo said.

The badger started to speak again but got frustrated quickly. "Taw-ck haerd." The badger shuffled forward and put its paws to the computer console. It had long, curved claws that clattered against the keys on the keyboard as it typed. But, it typed fast. Words spilled across the computer screen in a voice much more like the one that had reached out to Gerangelo asking for help originally.

"The keepers don't know I can type. They don't know I can use the computer. They didn't like it when I tried to talk to them, so I've kept it secret. I found information about you on the intrastellar info-net. I know you help robots prove their sentience, and I believe I'm sentient. I know I'm not a robot, but I can't find anyone who helps people like me. Please, help."

Gerangelo stared at the words on the screen. These were not the words of a quasi-sentient. They were the coherent, well-reasoned words of a full-sentient. He looked at the badger-like creature again. It was staring up at him with hope in its eyes. Not the blind-faith hope of one of the dumb pets that humans kept on Crossroads Station. This was the considered, delicate, easy-to-break hope of a creature who was fully aware that hope could be crushed.

There was no real choice here. There was only one right thing to do, no matter how little Gerangelo liked it.

"What's your name?" Gerangelo asked. One of the first questions in the sentience tests. Respondents didn't have to have a name to prove their sentience—but they had to give a considered response to the question.

"Zhey cawl Nanny Beahr." The badger-like creature shook its head. "Nawt like zhat. Ai cawl...Nahn-see."

"Nancy?" Gerangelo asked, checking he'd understood right.

The badger creature nodded eagerly. "Saw in vid, fouwnd ohn info-net."

"You spend a lot of time on the info-net when the keepers aren't around?" Gerangelo asked.

Nancy nodded. "Yooo halp?"

Gerangelo smiled grimly. "Yes, I'm going to help you. Are there any others here like you?"

"Nawt shure," Nancy said. "Nawt zhis roooom."

Gerangelo would have to get a warrant to check the entire place out, including their projects under development. That could wait. For now, he needed to get Nancy out of here. He held out a hand—perfectly designed to mimic a human's hand, right down to the creases and veins in the skin, all artificial of course—and took ahold of Nancy's coarse paw.

Nancy had rough paw pads under her crescent claws. At first, she seemed surprised by the robot man's gesture, but then her paw squeezed his hand. He knew how to comfort organics. That had been part of his original programming, and it would always be with him. He smiled at her again, more softly, and her eyes sparkled with gratitude. Someone had finally listened to her.

Gerangelo led Nancy back through the gengineered rainforest. He found himself wondering whether the trees would develop sentience and come crying to him for help next. When he got back to Laura and Jeffa, he said, "I've found what I was looking for."

"Excuse me?" Laura asked with an intonation so similar to the one Nancy had used to get Gerangelo's attention that he could hear the influence the keeper woman had had on the developing creature—an unintentional mother, cold and uncaring. Laura didn't think of Nancy as a person, and would never have seen her as a child—only a product.

But, Nancy might well have seen the keepers here as parents of a sort. She had limited alternatives, given the banks of test tubes and incubators Gerangelo had seen in the lower laboratories.

Gerangelo used his free hand to pull a digi-comp out of his pocket and held it forward so Laura could inspect it. "I'm a licensed member of the Sentience Board, and I believe GENE-TECH has been harboring sentients here without affording them their full rights."

"We don't have any robots," Jeffa woofed. His triangular ears had splayed out in bewilderment.

"I didn't say robots." Gerangelo gritted his teeth. Organics were so imprecise. It drove him crazy. "I said *sentients*, and the Sentience Board doesn't specify that applicants to the sentience tests be robots." He looked down at the badger creature holding his hand. He was developing a fondness for her, simply from seeing how much she must have struggled through to reach out to him. She had rewritten herself as a person in her own eyes, in spite of being raised to see herself as...nothing. "I believe that Nancy here qualifies for an initial examination."

"But the Nanny Bear Project and its prototype is the property of one of our biggest investors!" Laura exclaimed. Her eyes flashed with anger.

"Sentients are never property," Gerangelo said. "So your contract with your investor became null and void when Nancy developed sentience. Assuming she has. Check my credentials."

Gerangelo tilted his head to the side as he watched Laura and Jeffa study the credentials in his digi-comp. Their faces showed increasing frustration. They could see that their company was in trouble, and there was nothing they could do about it.

"We'll have to double-check all of this," Jeffa woofed.

"Of course," Gerangelo said. His authority in this realm was ironclad. Though it might take a few hours for the bureaucracy here to realize that, come to terms with it, and release him to take Nancy back to Crossroads Station on his shuttle.

Humans were a strange lot. They made rules, like sentience must be respected in all forms, and then they strained against following those same rules. It was bad programming.

"In the meantime—" Gerangelo looked back down at Nancy, still gripping his hand tightly with her fuzzy brown paw. "—would you like to show me around...your home?" He had no desire to examine this hideous rainforest further, but Nancy needed a chance to say goodbye to her stifling cradle.

He'd be introducing her to a whole new world—a whole universe full of possibilities—shortly. He had no doubts she would pass the sentience tests and become a full citizen of the Human Expansion. The sentience tests were not hard to pass, not if an individual truly wanted to pass them.

The true test of self-awareness is the belief that you have it. And Nancy—although not a robot—was one of the most compelling examples of emergent sentience that Gerangelo had ever seen.

The Witch Road

Dawn Trowell Jones

Dawn Trowell Jones lives in Atlanta, Georgia, but grew up on the southern coast of South Carolina. She writes speculative fiction. Her works have appeared in Typehouse Literary Magazine and Mysterical-E. She has a short story on Kindle (an alien-encounter sci-fi short story, The Secha, pronounced SESH-uh, or whatever you like). She tweets—

@DawTrowJo—and posts on her blog at dawntrowelljones.com.

Tempie wrapped the straws around the rock as fast as her fingers could work them.

The mayor didn't ordinarily visit them. She'd never seen one up close before. Even now, as she wove the straws, it was only his pasty nose when he leaned into the gap. Murmurs from the townsfolk who'd accompanied him out sifted in on a grainy evening umber.

Waving the gnats from her face, Mama glanced down at Tempie with Cale on the floor, stepped outside, and shut the door. Dana, their sister, stopped fixing supper and moved in close to listen. It was twilight out, and the crickets were dinning something fierce.

"Back *off* me, Cale. Let me finish, *then* you can see." Eyeing Dana, Tempie elbowed her brother, and prepared to wrap the next rock.

A toy for Cale; it was supposed to be old Sam, the donkey the Cohens used to haul their smoked venison to town. As water-bearer, she'd toted through town plenty of times and felt she had a proper sense of Sam—head, body, legs, tail—but now she wished she'd spent more time in the fish markets with the weavers. Last winter, when the fire got good and bright, she'd lie back all dreamy, stare at Mama's marrying baskets, and contemplate weaving. But there wasn't a fire now, just the flicker of the one sewing candle.

Unable to resist anymore, she set the frayed donkey down and jumped up to listen.

Mama was *sobbing.*

What on earth made Mama cry? Not even when she'd burned her hand that day did she cry like that. But, no, not so, she did, once, when the babies in her belly died: before Cale, there'd been boys, twins, born tiny and twisted, and Papa'd had to bury them out back by the azaleas, stabbing the black sandy dirt while Tempie'd hid and watched.

With mounting dread, it dawned on her; why the coming of the mayor, the townsfolk, Mama's crying. Her voice cracked high and distant like lightning in a dry summer's storm.

"Dana, *why's* she cryin' like that?"

Papa should have been back by now.

"I'm gonna go ask," Tempie said and sprang at the door.

Dana caught her by the wrist. Though strong for her size, at ten, Tempie couldn't put up much of a fight against a big sister, sixteen and grown.

Still holding onto her sister's wrist, Dana slumped, while on the other side of the door, the mayor spoke loud enough for everyone to hear.

"There's but one thing to do, Dolores. Make the pledge. Quick, ya hear? No point drawin' it out. She came up yesterday, was askin' 'bout your girl, funny enough, but then that's what you'd expect of the Waysegger. Returnin' in a few weeks' time. It's best for your *family*, given the situation, and you'd be doing right by our community. We take care of those who make an offering, Dolores. You know *that*."

Feet shuffled on the gritty planks.

"I'll think on it, Mayor...It was kind of you all to come," Mama said, her voice scarcely a sound. "Couldn't have been easy on you folks."

***

The kitchen was a hot swamp of savory smells. Cale loitered at the table, brushed by Mama's skirt as she scraped tubers and the rest. Weeks had passed since the mayor's visit, and they had little left to eat.

"Can't I help?"

"I done told you what to do. Do *nothing*. Not this night. *Please*, child, for the love of the Goodly Ghost, come comfort Caleb. Your sisters and I have it."

Since the news about Papa, he'd near sucked his donkey to shreds, and his thumb looked like a pale, sickly prune. Tempie slapped it out of his mouth, and his big black eyes needled her with vexation.

"He *knows*, Mama," she said, half to herself, woozy with validation.

"Knows *what*? Girl, I swear, do you have to say everything that pops into your head?"

Cale clutched his donkey.

Not a bad hold, Tempie thought anxiously, as her mind tried to run two tracks at once. But a few straps of Sharah's fabric might stop the legs from bending the wrong way...

The fact was, since Papa's death, there'd been this terrible ache in her gut that hurt worse than hunger and often made her too sad to think. *Maybe when I get big,* she used to say when circumstances overwhelmed, but she wasn't big, not yet, not within a few weeks' span. But maybe the old Witch would show her how to *do* more, still words, make something paltry plentiful or someone weak strong, for that was where they meant to send her, though nobody said, just a baleful look every now and again.

But she already had a notion of how to still the words. Given enough time, maybe she could figure the rest out.

They should have named me Tempest. They say the right name can make a person, and then all you gotta do is scratch any old mark on a scrap of wood so long as it's always the same mark for the same sound—that's how the olden-day scribes must have done it...

In Tempie's fantasy, she could almost write her name: If you can write your name, you'll live forever, better than any Waysegger Witch! Many times, she'd eyed that dreary lane; it was where the offerings went, people said: a long, lonely trek down a dusty road. But I'll be brave, she thought rather arbitrarily.

Steam pumped from a pot; next to it, dough to be cooked with their last slab of salt-pork.

"What *I* want," Mama began, but then she wiped her cheek with the back of her hand. "I want you to remember me, not as a mother who failed you, but the mother who knew that you, above all others, could survive this."

Of course, as the youngest girl, it had to be her. It was fate coming, fate coming for *her* this time, a second seismic shift to her short life. Papa had had such warm, thick-padded hands. Ever since his disappearance, Tempie's brain had flashed images of what they might have done to those hands...

Bread sizzled. Mama didn't say more, but her broad back heaved. Papa was gone. *Utterly* gone. The guns were gone, too, as they belonged to the town. Like one of those old boat docks undermined by a fateful change in current, the family was no more.

Papa'd left to confront Red Raiders on a neighboring isle. Townsfolk paid the Fringemen to fend off Raiders, but Papa and the men like him were expected to look after their own. All anyone knew was that the Raiders had sprung a trap. Papa was lost.

"Sit," Mama said once supper was laid out, "Sit. I want you all to sit down. You, too, Caleb."

All except Cale took seats around the table, which seemed lopsided with no whiskered Papa at the head. Tempie clambered into Papa's chair since nobody else would and folded her legs up under her. Cale meandered to her side.

"I can't make it," Mama announced. "You know that I can't. I *prayed* to the Goodly Ghost and I prayed...And I can't pray no more. There's nothing to be done. I made the pledge."

"But *look* at her," said the eldest. "She's a *pup.*"

"Lay off, Edie." Never one to sit still, Dana stood up again and wiped her hands on her one good dress. "Tell us, then, Mama," she said from the kitchen, gathering specks of flour. "What did the Waysegger say when you offered up our Tempie?"

Tempie's scalp pricked.

Tell me, Mama, tell me: "Papa's dead as a doornail, girl, and I've gone and pledged you to the Waysegger!"

Cale—Tempie could scarcely look at him so warm and quiet at her elbow, with his nasty wrinkled thumb and clingy hands that were always tugging at her smock, getting in the way of the work of her feet. She hadn't thought of him—a smack in the face, really, because she'd hardly thought at all. With her gone, who'd care for *him*?

"Like I said, I done it." Mama sighed. "Thanks be to the Goodly Ghost, she'll take them."

Like a bat had bit her, Sharah looked up from her lap.

"*Sharah?*" said Dana, genuinely shocked. "But she's been promised...You sayin' you gave the Waysegger *me*?"

"The Waysegger is to take Temperance...And...she's gonna take Caleb, too."

"What?" Edie said, indignant. "We're not *that* bad off, are we? He's the *boy*."

Tempie'd seen the Waysegger up close, once, from behind: torn rags for a dress, clanky chicken bones in her hair, a stooped back. The protruding parts of her crumpled face showed whenever the old Witch turned her head. Should Fringefolk find themselves in a pitiful state, when 'the Ghost's got no more givin' to give,' the Waysegger paid the town a premium in healthy seeds, tools, and goats for a single apprenticing girl. It was hard to grow crops in blighted soil, people said. When denied a pledge, the Witch wouldn't return for a long spell, even years, and that was a very bad thing.

But Tempie refused to be afraid, not of an old Witch, not Raiders, not *nothing*.

"You're mine now, mine *alone!*" Mama bellowed. "No Fringe woman has ever supported a family on scrap. We're the Unlucky, the shunned, won't survive the winter without Thomas. And if we hunt for ourselves, *daughters*, they'll hammer us in. We'll *burn*. I refuse to see you starve! *Won't!* It's the little ones who suffer the worst. Don't you *know* that? Behind closed doors, unimaginable pain, bellies bloated like a carcass 'bout to blow. So don't think of putting on a brave face for *them*. It's done. Might be the first great sacrifice of *your* young lives. Out here on the Fringe, won't be your last!"

Flushed and sweaty, Mama spread her legs and frowned at Tempie across the table.

Tempie grabbed hold of Cale's head, meaning to comfort him— but she'd pushed his curls into his eyes, and he shoved her off to resume his voracious thumb-sucking.

"Take care of m'boy, Temperance. Don't be a burden to the Waysegger. Said she knows who you are, seen you with those water jugs, gawking behind. I told her you'd never leave without Caleb, so she said she'll take him, *special*. Town's got no use for a girl like you. A pity, that, I suppose."

It was the last of the food stores, and nobody ate. Supper congealed while Mama stared sightless at the empty space on the wall where her marrying baskets had hung. Tempie felt it, felt it to her core: what life Mama'd had in her was thoroughly spent. In Papa's chair, knees tucked under her chin, Tempie gazed upon her three sisters, their fretful faces, each in turn, as if from the outside looking in, like she'd become a man grown, a Papa, and they were the frail ones who needed protecting. But when she found Cale, her stomach lurched.

***

At the first blue tinge of morning light, Tempie rolled out of her hammock and slipped out the back door. She'd borrowed Sharah's needle and thread and brought an empty spice jar Mama didn't see her swipe. Tempie'd often heard the Witch took small offerings, too, frogs and butterflies and weeds, and during her day-long totes as water-bearer, she'd imagined what she might give the old Witch if she ever needed to curry favor. Something *dreadful*. Something that showed nerve.

Tempie walked up to the plank of knotty wood Papa'd said wouldn't do for the pen; he'd told Edie not to waste it, hang it high and not leave it on the ground where critters would nest and baby Cale might toy with it. But Edie'd never got round to hanging the plank. It'd always seemed so forlorn, left there to rot. And Papa'd been right: one day, Cale did get a hold of it, a day when Tempie forgot to watch close. Strong for his dimply arms, Cale'd pushed the plank over, and sure enough, underneath lay fifty or so shiny black beads, any one of which could kill a man miserably. Seeing what Cale'd done, Tempie'd poked them to see them swarm, but overcome with the willies, she'd knocked the plank back. Today, when the sun rose high enough, she'd be ready...

***

Cale refused to leave. Always, *always*, he'd dogged her heels, but today of all days, he dragged his feet, sandals on but whimpering, until Mama picked him up whole-bodied and placed him like a doll out front at the gate where Tempie stood and waited. Tempie patted the warm jar in her pocket—inside, the necklace of shiny black beads. The legs had already ceased twitching by the time she'd dropped the necklace in: it was a different sort of nervousness she felt now.

Mama and each of her sisters stiffly kissed her goodbye. All hugged Cale tight until he grew fussy, but then Dana got down on her knees and embraced Tempie again.

"But Mama, won't it take *days* to get there?" Tempie said, rubbing her eyes. "You don't have *nothing* for us to eat?"

"No, child, but you won't need it. This is the way of things. You'll see."

***

During the night, Tempie'd had doubts; this was why she wanted her jar of black beads, and now that she and Cale had actually left, looking at his unhappiness, she shuddered. This was wrong. He shouldn't be with her. Cale didn't eat much, and there'd be more food soon.

But Mama was mama, and she'd made the pledge.

The day's heat wasn't fully on them yet, but they would reach town before midday, and for this reason at least, Tempie stuck to the plan.

But she considered another plan.

"Quit dragging them feet, Cale!" she shouted back at the boy, who skulked along, glowering, the grass-and-stone donkey in his hand.

Veering north had more than once crossed her mind. They could head to Wah'bro instead, maybe live up there until Cale grew big and made his own family. It was a world away and foreign, but the villagers there didn't know she wasn't a witch. Maybe she could wave her arms a bit like old Waysegger, dress herself in rags, tell people their business, and take offerings—and until that day, people always needed fresh water, didn't they?

But she didn't *know* the plan would work. What if Wah'bro had its own Waysegger? And though she could run far and eat little and survive hidden in barns, Cale couldn't run worth squat and fussed too much. Mama and her sisters would starve. The town would suffer.

Like a squirrel caught in an osprey's shadow, her thoughts leapt round and round. On the road from Windlass Point, they passed under moss-draped elms, prickly palms, and sprawling oaks. Dust from the road coated her throat, while Cale trudged along, eerily quiet, falling farther and farther behind.

The day was getting hot.

Crickets murmured in the brush as the sun crept high above the rustling canopy. She didn't cry, but kicked the short grass between the wheel ruts while Cale jogged to catch up. A deerfly buzzed her ear.

"Come *on*...Look...you've got to pay attention to the world, Cale. It's your *job* now. See? I'm giving you a job. Take them trees. You know how when it rains and puddles, and after a while, the puddles are gone? It's the trees sucking up *all* that water. It's like... it's like they're trying to give it back, but don't know how, can't reach high enough. And when they grow big and tall, they're just raining upward, except *real* slow. You gotta pay attention to the world, Cale, and see the truth in things, even when the truth is long and thin."

Having caught up, Cale pulled his thumb from his mouth, and

put his hand in hers. For a long time, they walked together hand in hand.

They were already thirsty when Farmer Rosta approached; back from town, his swayback mare pulled a flatbed full of supplies. Tempie'd hauled water for Rosta during last year's drought and now eyed the sloshing yellowed jugs in his flatbed. The heavy cart creaked to a stop. Rosta studied both her and Cale sharply, but instead of offering a sip from a jug, he handed them a small glass bottle.

Sheathed in leather with a strap to hang around the neck, the bottle was filled with water clear as crystal and stoppered with cork. Tempie carefully took a sip and helped Cale to a sip, who was already red in the face. The bottle only held a few sips, so she passed it back to old man Rosta, but he mimed for her to drape it around her neck. Then, as if he'd been expecting them, he rummaged in his shoulder-pack and handed each a hard roll. Thus done, he tipped his frayed hat and tugged at the mare's lead, which set the wheels of the flatbed to turning.

"Stick close when we get to town," Tempie said, nervous, and they ate their rolls.

***

The roadside thickets started to clear as they hit the outskirts of town, where they passed three crumbling walls overrun with kudzu; an old ruin called the Mushroom Fac'try, people said it used to have its own special road for steel-wheeled carriages, before folks tore it up. There was an old chipped painting of one inside the alehouse—she'd snuck in once to see it—but nobody she knew had ever seen such a beast in *real* life. They belonged to the days of old, hundreds of years gone, and people turned awful hush when talk of the olden days cropped up.

"Look, there's the castle, Cale, waitin' for the ghost train. Not the Goodly Ghost, *lonesome* ghosts...Means we're about there... But I was thinking..." The road to Wah'bro connected midway down Main Street, and the words just spilled off her tongue: "There's another way we could take, other than the Witch Road. You probably don't know about Wah'bro, but it's just a town. So, which you want?"

The boy reclaimed his thumb and blinked at her.

"It's me and you, Cale. *We* didn't make the pledge. But, Old Waysegger, maybe she ain't be so bad. Wise, they say. Powerful. Everyone respects a witch, Cale, it's just most don't want to live with one. Saw her up close, once. *Sure* was ugly...Now, don't be scared, it don't mean nothing...Got kind of a puffy face." Tempie pressed her own thin cheeks to show what she meant. "And this dried-up gray hair, and sweats funny, too, if you look close. You have to look *real* close sometimes, Cale. Don't forget. And she smells like pickles. How a body gets to smelling like pickles, I do *not* know."

Cale took Tempie's hand again and soon they crossed a ring of tall, pastel-splashed houses as they entered the first shady streets of town.

People stopped and stared as they passed, for unlike her usual, she was without a shoulder pole and escorted by a small boy— but soon several hurried to their carts, rummaging the way Rosta had done. Then they came: from shops and homes, carrying rolls, pastries, and sweets, bursts of flavor that tickled the brain—she'd never tasted *anything* so fine. Most brought fancy small water bottles on leather straps, corked like Rosta's—except for two sheathed in silver. And the townsfolk kept on coming, hanging more and more bottles on her neck till they became right burdensome, and they had to start piling a few on Cale. By the time she and Cale had made it across town center, she was turning people down, and their faces went dark with concern.

In the ruckus, the townsfolk had ushered them far past the road to Wah'bro, without the slightest chance of doubling back unscen.

There it was. A large structure had long ago disintegrated, leaving among the scattered blocks of rubble, sour grass, and scrub trees, a single massive arch where the deep, sandy soil of the Witch Road extended pale and narrow between its posts. All that indicated where their solitary journey was to begin was that one isolated arch, a barrier that didn't have any kind of substance to keep a person in or out—a useless sort of gatekeeping, to Tempie's mind.

Still, nobody followed them under the arch, and too quickly, they passed out of its shade.

Bottles clinked.

No branches overhung the Witch Road. It baked in utter brilliance under a cloudless sky.

Cale looked tired, but his little feet chugged along. Tempie was tired, too. She wished they'd rested awhile before entering town and all the fuss, maybe under some leafy magnolia, anything with shade, even an airy bush would have done the job. But as hungry and thirsty as they'd been, once in town, it was too late. And it was definitely too late now, for there was no breeze on the Witch Road, nor shade at all, only wide-open exposure under a vivid blue.

The crickets didn't care, chirruping their low hymns in the scrub brush.

It was late afternoon. Hours had passed of hot sand sifting

into their sandals, sizzling their toes, until she noticed Cale had stopped, and found him fiddling with one of the bottles at his neck.

"Hold up, now, Cale. We can't go drinking it all too fast."

Dumbly, his red-hot face squinted up at her; he popped the bottle open and drank its contents.

She was getting right sick of her own voice. A deerfly buzzed menacingly. Lord, if it bites him, I'll hear peals, for sure.

"Shoo, bug! Go!"

Her brother uncorked another bottle and tilted it back for the precious liquid. Sweat beaded his forehead. Her own head ached something fierce, so she drank a couple of the bottles, too.

For hours, they walked. Far in the distance, the nearest trees looked hazy like the dim mural of the train. Mid-afternoon was the hottest part of the day—every child knew that when the sun hit that particular mark, it was time to get inside quick and find a cool floor: a bare back on cold dirt felt heavenly.

A thought kept gnawing at her: Where did all the offerings go? *That's* what she wanted to know. Nobody ever accompanied the Waysegger *back* to town; the witch came alone, always, except after an offering, but it was only her pony who travelled with her, drawing the rickety cart filled with goods.

She hoped the pretty bottles held enough. Cale cracked open another.

"Just that one, Cale. Okay?"

"O-kay," he said, and drained it.

"Wish someone had thought to give us hats. Two hats." Her feet slid in the soft sand. "Wait...I've got an idea. Let's tear up some of that tall grass."

With his dirty feet splayed and his stomach poked out, Cale blinked at his sister.

"Fine. I'll do it. You rest."

She snatched up grass from the side of the road and when she had a fistful tried fanning Cale with it to test her plan, which didn't seem too effective, but then she tried spreading out the fronds so that they might at least work as a hat. Like with the donkey, she looped them for better shape and stiffness.

"Hold it over your head. Like this."

Cale did as he was told, but his arms were too short and his head too big, and it simply wasn't going to work. Tempie tried to think what she could do. Cale's face was too red.

"Drink another of your bottles, Cale. Go on. Forget what I said. No, that's all right...I'll wait a bit for mine."

The boy chugged the water without wasting a drop, squeezing his eyes tight as if his whole existence had distilled into this one act, the most exquisite pleasure he'd ever known. Disgusting to watch.

"Let's put your shirt over your head, but put it back on when the sun dips."

They walked on.

They couldn't hear the ocean but passed low-lying mud where saltwater had pooled close to the road. White trees, dead, wavered in the distance across a field of brown chord grass. The ocean had drowned them, and she was reminded of tales Papa'd told of miles and miles of slender sun-bleached branches thrusting out of the sea to pierce the hulls of unwary fishermen, ghostly white boughs creaking in the water's green. But on land crabgrass grew just about everywhere, and here it clawed thick along the sand, so it seemed a lucky thing the road wasn't shrinking away at the sides like the trunks and boughs of all those withered trees...

***

Night dribbled in, a watery purple haze, and as soon as it was too dark to see, they lay down in warm, milky sand and coiled their arms around their heads to keep critters off. Orphaned noises sounded in the wild. Tempie wrapped herself around her brother as best she could, hoping nothing was padding its way through the gloom to claw at her unwatched back.

"Don't worry," she whispered in his ear, and fell into a dreamless sleep.

***

The morning was misty and still as they drank two bottles each to calm their empty stomachs. But once the sun had climbed high enough, the crickets commenced screaming all over again, one batch raising the chorus just as the other fell off. Tempie's knees ached worse than ever. Her head pounded. Step by aching step, nothing but sand, and grass, and the roar of crickets, which by some miracle stayed invisible under the unrelenting glare of the sun. Cale moved slower at midday, and by afternoon, looked about ready to wail.

They'd travelled far down the Witch Road and now had only three full bottles left. Low in the horizon's shimmer, there appeared a faint billowy tree. Tempie didn't feel a breeze, but there ahead was the promise of relief, and this small gift made her happy. A saltmarsh was shaped like a bowl, so maybe a gap in the forest was funneling in fresh air. But she feared this was just another mirage and blinked and blinked until her eyes grew sore—yet still, she saw a billowy tree, ahead to the left, gently swaying.

There wasn't just the one tree, either, but two, one bunched behind the other, both alone yet somehow together in the mealy wasteland.

Cale began to whimper. They stopped and drank while Tempie eyed the two trees and their greenly mellifluent limbs.

Bottles clinked. Empty bottles clinked louder than full ones.

But this, this was *worse* than scrap-land—what crops could grow here? What sort of person lived in the middle of a marsh under a blazing-hot sun?

A witch, that's who.

But a witch was powerful, wasn't she? Then, what were two small children going to be able to do for a witch that a witch couldn't do for herself—or for that matter, that any of the other offerings couldn't do? Offerings were supposed to learn from the Waysegger, to become like her. People said. Where *were* they?

What did Mama do?

"Hey! See them *two* trees ahead?" Tempie said abruptly, heart racing.

Cale didn't answer.

The empty bottles were a burden, but valuable, and Tempie was afraid to leave them behind. Nevertheless, she found herself scanning the gnarly crabgrass for broken bottles like theirs, choked with mud, or a dainty silver sheath, half-crushed. Sun-bleached bone.

Time passed, thick and slow.

"Cale? Do you see them trees?" she said again, after a while.

"Uh huh," Cale replied, which startled her. He took out his thumb and gestured ahead: "Uh tree."

"No, two trees. Two."

Cale looked again, stuck his thumb in his mouth, and glanced up at his sister, waiting. His face sagged funny.

"See how close they are? That's what you call *entwined*. Like a... like a mama and her baby. Or, more like a prince and his princess, happy together. *Entwined*. Like the pieces of your donkey.

"And you see...there was a prince and a princess, *once*, and this prince and princess, they weren't royalty like folks in the heart-fire-tales Papa tells...uh, told. No, they were poor folk, *Fringe*-folk, like *us*. A boy and a girl. And the village's mayor, he sent them on a great mission to save the village from Raiders, because in *their* village, little girls and boys always had worth. Both could fight...In fact, they could swap chores if they didn't like their chores and wanted to swap...

"So, these two went on a *mission*, and the Witch that guarded the village—What? *Ours*? No, no, some other witch. Maybe the Waysegger's *great*-great-grandmother. This was a long time ago, Cale. Anyway, the Witch, she swooped up through the mosses and out of the starry blackness, to where the prince and princess hid under a bush, because the Raider Chief had taken the whole village now and the Raiders were going to cook 'em up on *huge* spits, and eat their juicy hands and juicy feet..."

Cale whimpered, stopped walking. Tempie turned to him.

"And the Witch said, 'Come with me, and I'll save you from your peril. Your village is lost. Everyone will die. But I'll make you into trees down a long and lonesome road. You'll grow tall and strong and chock-full of majesty...And nobody will chop you up and make you burn, and you'll be together like this—like *that*, Cale—for as long as you live, which will be the terribly long life of a tree. You'll be safe from others in a wide field of grass and thickets. You'll have delicious rainwater and salty breezes. But the saltwater won't ever reach you on *my* road and turn you white, because it's *my* road, the Witch Road, and I protect all who travel it.'" Tempie waved her arms grandiosely.

"Thi' road?" squeaked Cale around his thumb.

"This very road, and there they *are*. Proof! The prince and princess, locked in wood, where they live on forever as a story told by children. Only children know *this* story, Cale. Only children know how the Witch protects these trees from harm, to mark the way to her happy huts, where there's food and fresh water and she-goats for little boys to play with. While their sisters work hard all day. I'll work *hard*, all day, for you, Cale. Just for you."

Her eyes stung, squinting in the bright sun.

"And I'm not making any offerings, either. Except for my black beads here."

Cale reinserted his thumb.

The road wound to the right as the trees came closer. Wow,

they must be really tall, Tempie thought, but lacked anything for scale.

Her thoughts drifted.

"Ever notice how if you take 'hog' and 'dog,' you only get a different sound at the beginning?" Her knees ached so bad, she thought she might collapse. "It's...like a leaf boat on the big puddle back home. You say 'hog' and it's like blowing at it, and saying 'dog' is sort of like pushing, only with your tongue...And you know what? I could make any old mark on a slab of driftwood, just to say, just to say I *mean* 'og' or...or...Oh, I dunno...Why'd anyone mean 'og'?"

Farther down the road, they moved, closer and closer to the trees. Her knees ached so bad, she thought she might collapse. And her *heart* ached; it ached to see those lush branches weaving into one another. It was a story she'd told Cale to make him feel safe, but it had made *her* feel safe—and that was how things needed to be. Particularly now that the water was gone.

But the angle was off. The nearer they got, the more obvious it was that she'd been wrong about her trees sitting by the road; they were far from it; and after a while, Cale began whimpering again, pointing ahead. Tempie saw it, too. A warbling figure in the late afternoon haze. Though a fair distance from the trees, it seemed to be getting closer. Her spirits lifted, and she grabbed Cale's hand.

"If that's someone up there, we're apt to meet by the trees." Then to herself, she whispered: "Do the trees ever get lonely?"

It did look like somebody coming, or maybe *two* somebodies coming down the road, dribbling in the heat mirages: one short and one tall. But her head pounded with a vicious thirst. With each step, the phantom-people lost cohesion, and so did her hopes.

But no! No! The trees! Once closer, her perspective shifted again: the trees, they'd pulled apart. And they didn't sway at all, but stood stock still; the fresh breeze had been an illusion, and the air was as putrid and sweltering as ever. She let go of Cale's hand.

A fly buzzed.

When they reached a point in the bend parallel to the trees, Tempie stopped and slumped, mind choked from heat and thirst. It was obvious that an enormous gulf stood between the trees' closest branches. Not entwined at all, prince and princess, mother and child, nobody embraced anybody; they remained forever yearning across an empty field as fat and dry as her swollen tongue. She'd believed in her story, needed to, and now, with its diminishment came her own: "*Liars! You liars!*"

Dammed-up grief overflowed, and oblivious to everything, Tempie sobbed as never before, for her family, her home, her life. All phantoms, all gone. A gulf of space and time, as impassable as what lay between those unmoving trees, severed her from everything she'd ever known. Cheeks smeared with bitterness, there were to be no more pleasures of mundane wonderment. Every choice held the direst consequences; every comfort summoned treachery; and here she was, just a girl, and a fool, not the savior of her fantasies, not smart enough to have seen the truth in time...

That she'd been leading them to their deaths.

When the Ghost's got no more giving to give...give unto the Waysegger!

"No, no, *no*, you're not *goodly* at all! You're a stingy one, you Ghost! Mama! *Mama!* She failed us, Cale! She *failed* us! I *swear*, if God *is*, and God is *good*, then God is good for *God*. That's it. Wasn't ever about us...I just wanted to be good for *us*."

Transfixed by the dull listlessness of the trees, dead to her now, Tempie hadn't noticed Cale thrusting his donkey at something ahead in the road. Brain baked, she didn't want to know *things* anymore—she was about to vomit.

But she turned to see what upset him.

There was a girl in the road, clearly now, knobby knees locked, black-haired and back-lit, which seemed strange. There was something bulky on her chest, shiny, and she too shaded her eyes while glaring suspiciously at Tempie and Cale. The girl was thin and didn't say hello, but the dirty little boy next to her tipped his head. An object flopped in his hand...

Tempie dropped her hands from her eyes.

The girl did the same.

What's this?

Thoughts were looping fast—she glanced to the left again, at the moveless trees. But not *trees*, there was only one tree—the sea of dry chord grass that surrounded them had been so similar-looking, created so much sameness, that even now it was impossible to make out the mirror's breadth, only that it was larger than anything Tempie could ever have imagined.

It emitted a peculiar tinny hum.

Bang. They jumped, and their bottles clinked.

The mirror cracked, and Tempie grabbed Cale's hand, ready to bolt. It split down the center, dividing the air and their reflections in a perfectly straight line—a *rift*. The hum shifted pitch, and within the spreading gap, there appeared a recessed set of steps that led up.

Above the top step, more blue sky, but not the same sky as what lay behind them, what they'd followed for days. This was the world beyond the veil!

A person stepped into the aperture: a body filled it but the head was unseen. And then, the person pivoted as if to signal to someone who stood off to the side. Another step down, and the head emerged, crowned with a dark mass of reddish-brown hair. Not a man, but a woman, she wore a long coat over a sleek jumpsuit, both immaculately white, and when she reached the lowest step and her face dropped fully into daylight, it glowed with the healthiest sheen Tempie'd ever laid eyes on.

The woman beckoned them to come.

Even if they'd wanted to run, there was nowhere to go. Cale returned Tempie's tight grasp.

Decision made, Tempie wiped her splotchy face and marched them straight across the final stretch of hot, gritty sand to the waiting Waysegger—for standing before them was the Witch for sure, only not so old without the puffiness and the grayness and with all the waxy sweat washed away.

You've got to pay attention to the world, Tempie thought, heart fluttering with anticipation. You have to see the truth in things.

One step up, and she led her little brother out of that dusty realm into a shiny new one.

Ambassador Berry

Linda McMullen

Linda McMullen is a wife, mother, and American diplomat, most often found in Africa or Asia, but currently on a domestic rotation in Washington, D.C.

Linda's pieces have appeared or are forthcoming in Burningword, Typishly, Dragon Poet Review, and other publications. You can read her short story Elaine's Idyll at ojalart.com

Even in the early 2000s they could still grow strawberries in the Sahel; that's what my mother said. In her green eyes I saw, wafting through her crumbling memory palace, wisps of fruit eaten on the back of an underpowered *moto-taxi* in Ouagadougou. While a white woman on a prototypical, cliché-spewing, soul-searching trip across Africa, she at least had the decency to subvert the paradigm. Instead of going from Cape to Cairo, she went (as she said) "from the door of no return to the Horn." Dakar, then drifting eastward through Senegal, Gambia, Mali, Burkina Faso, sprinkling her passport with now-obsolete tattoos. She got as far as Ethiopia before she had no more dollars to convert to birr, and her parents' final offer was a ticket home. I turned up in the course of things; she bought me those now-rarefied fruits when there was a little money to hand back in Wisconsin.

She was, I think, a little dismayed when I became an ambassador.

"Starchy," she said. Her mind crackled in and out like a poorly tuned FM station, but I'm inclined to think that was the *mot juste*—for dutiful me, for my buttoned-down job.

She must have eaten those strawberries about sixty years ago.

Bowie says, "Ma'am, it's time."

Bowie—my communications expert, cum office manager, cum personal assistant—had introduced himself by declaring that his grandmother had seen *Labyrinth* one time too many, and christened him before anyone could intervene. He's a ferrety little man, on his first tour. He's eager as a Labrador, but the best one could hope for. In the circumstances.

I send an email back to Washington confirming our two-stop plan (I say, "plan"), then shut down my laptop, put it in its briefcase, and cede it to Bowie. We refresh the seals around the room. The dust will get in anyway.

"How many today?"

"Five."

His even tone fools neither of us. It means our night guards notified the rump national police force that a handful of souls perished in front of our embassy, asking for water. A slight hiccup on the vowel tells me what he hasn't said, that at least one of them had yet to walk. I have one semi-functional Bic left, and I set down on the wall, below yesterday's entry (seven):

July 2, 2052: Five souls.

"What's the point?" demands Lola. Her badge reflects the orange twilight trickling in through the translucent seals. "It's morbid."

I arch one eyebrow. She makes no attempt to obscure the sigh in her shoulders, retreats five feet to the door of my office, and knocks. *"Ma'am."* She glares at the tangerine light.

I refrain from all the things I could say—rumors about her last assignment, her office floor reportedly a kaleidoscope of green, blue, brown bottles—and remember that at least I'd volunteered for this. In some sense. "They're almost done," I say.

"That's what I came to tell you. Hank said they need more time."

"We don't have it."

She shrugs. "That's what he said."

Bowie says again, "Ma'am, it's time."

We lock the room. Bowie removes a threadbare handkerchief from his pocket—a delicate old-fashioned habit that never fails to amuse me—and mops his brow. We occupy a pocket of what used to be the U.S. Embassy in Ouagadougou, now dubbed the U.S. Mission in the Western Sahel, covering—as a practical matter—Mali, Niger, and Burkina Faso, and parts of Mauritania, Algeria, Tunisia, and Libya.

No matter what Toto said—or even Weezer—there are no more rains to bless down in this part of Africa.

I work out of the Ambassador's office; Bowie and Lola share the one opposite—the space formerly belonging to the Deputy Chief of Mission. Between—in what used to be an upscale reception area—is our living room/dining room/bedroom. It even includes a vestigial kitchen, with a bygone sink and microwave, and a tiny bathroom/shower (twenty years past functionality). We seal the offices at night to bring the central room down to a bracing seventy-eight. But I insist on using the offices during the day, eighty-five be damned; it's impossible to work in our unwashed fiasco of a flat.

The wind howls—six on the nose; Lola mechanically takes up her radio, calls to the guards. "Ça y est." It's their cue to seal up their posts and wait out the vespertine dust storm.

It's too early to eat.

Bowie goes into the safe, withdraws three bottles of water, and hands one to me and the other to Lola. "How much is left?" I ask.

Bowie just shakes his head. I count three remaining bottles.

My satellite phone rings, and I answer it. "Ma'am, it's Hank."

"How're things in sunny Tambao?" They're scratching manganese out of the ground. In industrial quantities.

"Slow," he says, curtly. "We've got our orders on tonnage, and –"

"We've got one more day," I say. "Washington emailed that they're sending the plane in."

"We need another week."

"We don't have it," I say.

That had become abundantly clear earlier this afternoon. We were down to our last quarter of a tank, and, per an irate Lola, the road temperatures were approaching 122°F. "I've seen what happens when the tarmac starts melting," she had said, without elaborating.

But I—over Bowie's and Lola's rare joint objection—had insisted on snaking my way to the guerilla leader's camp in our wheezing Suburban. He greeted us with a bright grin: he had been sucking on what I took to be a hard candy or cough drop, and it had stained his mouth vermillion. "Seigneur," I said. At least, I pretended I had heard him properly, and that was indeed the proper *nom de guerre* for Colonel Sanou, High Controller of the Airstrip and Uber Traficant in All Things Liquid. I hoped he was going for "his lordship" when he said *seigneur*. His pronunciation had edged toward "saigneur". *Bloodletter.* I had determined it was not in the interest of the U.S. government to inquire.

"We're going to be cutting it close," Hank barks.

"That's always been true."

Hank's *harrumph* rattles the receiver.

I say, "The plane will be here tomorrow. You and your men can be on it—or not."

There is little to say after that. Hank offers me the benefit of his unvarnished views anyway.

The blowing russet sand outside and the setting sun transform the light into a shade of gangrenous rust that never fails to put me off my dinner. "Eat," says Bowie, offering me an MRE. Meals ready to eat, officially. Meals ready to expectorate, in my view.

"Thank you," I say, setting it down.

"It's not any better tepid," says Lola.

The same conversations, looping like lazy flies.

I shouldn't say that. We've been here two months. I say, "I'll go lower the flag."

"I'll do it, Ma'am," says Lola. Every day.

Ambassador Marguerite Mae Vernon was the last to run a real mission here, back when the barrages still contained water and the "green belt" boasted patches of verdure—and the embassy itself held sixty Americans and three hundred local staff. Today the embassy walls still encase deep divots—the staff's primordial attempts at boreholes. (Bowie tore down an old cubicle and used the walls to cover them—"Safety first." He left the deepest one alone: when the moon is in the seventh house, and there's water close enough to the surface, *and* the pump works, we can procure a few buckets' worth. When that happens, Bowie bursts into my office, beaming: "Bath day!")

Before I came, I plowed through thirty years of old cables, and a few crumbling printed-out emails some prescient desk officer had saved. A then-Management Officer had contacted the mission in Cape Town to see how they had weathered (pun intended) the water crisis from 2015 onward. The Consulate General's chipper advice: bucket baths and—it now seems quaint—"if it's yellow, let it mellow." Then: decades of cables on local soil degradation read only by the State Department's environmental experts. After that: the local government's attempt to co-fund the Great Green Wall with the African Union, the Fulani peregrinations through Libya, or Algeria. More corpses in the Mediterranean, of course, but Washington's eyes were on the Strait of Hormuz.

But what held me rapt was Ambassador Vernon's first-hand account of the water skirmishes—a euphemistic name for the riots that began the current low-grade civil war—in a dashed-off email to her longtime friend and colleague, then the Assistant Secretary for African Affairs: "Adila—Military base is blazing—can hear screaming from here—whole town seems to be pillars of smoke. Contacts say tanks walling off the presidential palace and the television/radio stations—still trying to find out if in support of the government, or against. A quarter of the guards have fled. Currently fifty-four Americans at the embassy, all of us sheltering in place. All manning phones to reach other Americans in-country, but even SMS inconsistent. Have found about 150 wanting to leave. We'll keep trying. Supplies are short, particularly water, maybe four days left. Road to airport still open but reportedly fighting around the cathedral. Egyptians (nearby) have asked to be part of our convoy. Said yes.

Got to get local staff out this time, Adila. There are about 250 of them with their families, around 1300 total. There are pernicious and persistent rumors in the city that the embassy is hoarding water, and they'll be in grave danger. So: roughly 1500 Americans/embassy personnel to evacuate, and Egyptians (75?) likely to request air transport too. Explosions in the distance—gotta go –

M.M.V."

Ambassador Vernon pressed *send* milliseconds before the systems went down, and so didn't receive her friend Adila's response; she wasn't able to engage until an earsplitting and tearful satellite phone conversation a few days later. Adila, as the State Department's lead on all things Africa, had gone directly to the Secretary to convey the gravity of the situation. The Secretary was firm: there was no precedent for an "environmental" evacuation for staff, much less their families. Americans only.

State Department lore says Ambassador Vernon offered her old friend Adila some rather undiplomatic and biologically impossible advice for the Secretary. Adila reportedly agreed with the sentiment, but reminded Marguerite that she had a mission to lead. Marguerite reportedly retorted, "What the hell do you think I'm doing?" and hung up, thus annihilating a thirty-year friendship. Allegedly Ambassador Vernon saw the Americans settled, then tried to dash off the plane at the last moment—only to be sedated by the air crew.

Back in Washington, she refused the award the Department offered her, retired abruptly, and flew back. By that point around forty of the local staff had been murdered, along with several of their families. She spent the rest of her life trying to resettle the rest, or so the story goes. Supposedly she managed to save about five. Some say she too was murdered; some say she left this life completely insane.

I don't think it was either. She died ensuring that she could live with herself.

Lola comes back with the folded flag, that star-spangled triangle that still causes my heart to seize. "Thanks," I say, and finally ask the nagging question. "How do you always manage to fold that yourself? Isn't it a two-person job?"

She half-smiles. "My mom taught me."

"She must be a wonderful lady."

"She was," says Lola. Her tone discourages further questions, so I only say, "I'm so sorry."

"Thanks."

She looks younger, somehow, under her vinous rosacea —or maybe it's just that it's fading. We got through the remaining booze a month ago. She (and consequently we) had some exciting days afterward. "If you don't mind my asking," I say, "how old are you?"

"Thirty."

Thirty. Half a lifetime ago. "Why did you decide to join State?"

"It was a steady government job where people weren't shooting at me."

"But you joined Diplomatic Security," I point out, "and got yourself assigned to a danger-pay post."

"My mistake," she says. Our eyes meet.

I can't help grinning back at her.

I eat, and the three of us watch the far-off airport spotlight flickering. When the sandstorm has died down, it shines clear, and we venture out. Lola rolls her eyes when she sees my notebook.

The tarp covering the main checkpoint window has a tear, but the guards (apart from a dust patina) are fine. Bowie goes with Issa to determine what has become of the duct tape, while I glance toward Daouda. "J'en ai trois, Madame," he says, with a distinguished nod.

Three stories.

Daouda is the youngest son of Ambassador Vernon's head of protocol, killed by a thirsty mob in the days following her departure. The family actually delayed the memorial service until she returned; she gave the eulogy. Soon after we arrived, I brought Daouda a mostly-complete list of the local staff working for the embassy during Ambassador Vernon's tenure, and he, through his formidable social network, collects tidbits on their whereabouts. Many of them are untraceable, having made illicit treks north across the Sahara, or south to live (legally or otherwise) in Côte d'Ivoire. But some:

"He's in Bobo, working for the mayor."

"Dead from alcoholism."

"She's a teacher in Marseille."

Lola leans over my list. "Why? It's not like the Department's going to care."

"Someone will. Someday."

Sleep will find us, but not for an hour yet. Lola, Bowie, and I twist sweatily in our cots, failing to ignore the sour-breath smell of the room. "Truth or dare?" asks Bowie.

"Not again," says Lola.

Truth or Dare is a misnomer. Moving will make us warmer, so it's almost invariably Truth or Truth. "We're out of questions," I say. That is, they've asked everything that a serving ambassador can appropriately answer for her staff. Also, as I say, we're out of alcohol.

"C'mon," pleads Bowie. "None of us can sleep."

"Fine," says Lola; I can hear her scowl. "Truth."

"Worst move you've ever made."

Lola is silent, and I wonder if she'll refuse to answer. In a voice I almost don't recognize—"Our family was part of the Miami Migration. I remember salt water coming out of the tap one day. Mama shouted, 'That's it! We are *going*! Somewhere *nice*!'" She sighs. "We got as far as Coral Springs before the money ran out."

"That's pretty rotten," agrees Bowie.

"Truth or dare?" Lola says to Bowie.

"Dare," he says.

"I dare you to do a handstand," she says. Bowie—as usual—performs beautifully, this time walking around on his hands in the airport's spotlight gleam to liven up the execution. We applaud, dutifully.

"Not very creative," he says.

"It's your turn," she replies, flatly.

"Truth or dare, Ma'am?" he asks me.

"Truth." The truth is, even thirty years ago, I couldn't have done a handstand.

"Why did you take this assignment?"

What can I tell them that won't damage their fragile trust? That I aspired to see the word *Ambassador* in front of my name at the end of a long career, knowing my mother was fading, having parted ways with the notion of a family of my own, having mislaid my friends along the way? That the option was this or an ignominious retirement? That there was no one else willing to take on this dubious assignment?

"Because," I say, "at the end of the day, I took an oath to the Constitution of the United States."

Bowie makes a noise reminiscent of a *Jeopardy!* buzzer; Lola, an air horn. "Cop out," she says.

"Maybe," I reply, briskly. "Truth or dare."

"Truth," she says.

I consider returning the question, but that is cruel *and* a cop-out. "Favorite family member."

"My abuela," she says. There's an unprecedented catch in her voice; Bowie and I both shift toward her. "My dad wasn't in the picture. Mom was cashiering at Walmart, but it wasn't paying the bills. So she joined the army." She breathes. "I stayed with my abuela when she deployed. I was twelve...she didn't come back."

"I'm so sorry," I say again. It's just as pathetic this time.

Bowie says, sympathetically, "That sucks."

"Yeah," Lola says. "Truth or dare." A beat. "Ma'am."

"Truth."

"What are you most looking forward to at home?"

"Strawberries," I say.

The day doesn't so much dawn as hurl itself at us; the sand is a thing alive, flinging itself around the embassy. Tightening its silicon noose.

"It's the last day!" cries Bowie, when he sees me. He zips out of the room and goes outside to hoist the flag.

"Someone's in a good mood," says Lola, but the corners of her mouth lift a little. "We'll be back in the States soon."

"Yeah," I say. "Dome sweet dome."

She just shakes her head, and goes into the office she shares with Bowie.

It's already an old joke.

But that's why we're here, even if no one has said it out loud, or acknowledged it in any way. The water situation is...well-known; in the United States, air quality too has also gotten so bad that it's affecting even the wealthy. Still unwilling to recognize that any real public policy solutions were fifty to seventy-five years in the past, our Congress endorsed the next best thing: military contracting. Some combination of the Marine Corps of Engineers and the artist formerly known as Halliburton are encasing America's cities in giant geodesic domes.

Really.

Each will come equipped with giant purifiers to cleanse the air; the "panes" will be glass at the very bottom and semi-permeable membranes above; they're planning to monkey with the air pressure to allow the rain to trickle in, but reduce the amount of fresh water lost to evaporation. I could go on at length about the cost/ludicrousness of this "plan," but it was enacted under the state of emergency three years ago. Hadfield steel has come roaring back to life (American jobs!) and Tambao is the world's largest untapped source of manganese, its critical alloy. Congress is boasting that it has revived industry. I am here to oversee the evacuation of the miners and the precious manganese before the token local government collapses entirely.

And takes our fig leaf with it.

We pack our suitcases, and Bowie puts them in the car. I spend the day dry-mopping my office—an exercise Lola correctly identifies as pointless—and adding both the death tallies and Daouda's news of the former embassy staff to my journal. I remind Lola, pointedly, to go get the plane permits—a polite fiction that we and the residual government maintain. She goes. I log into my computer and read a few reporting cables from around the region. Embassy Abidjan's latest notes clashes between Burkinabé refugees and Ivoirian populations, and describes the precarious ethnic balance and upcoming elections as "a tinderbox in an already hot country." Embassy Algiers is reporting on sex trafficking among recent migrants...

I can't.

I move to turn it off. Time enough when we get back.

Before I can even touch the button, the power goes out.

We've been through this before, and there are only two options: opening the windows and choking on blowing sand, or keeping them closed and slow-roasting. We have a backup generator, but the (since-fired) Post Management Officer who equipped us refused to believe we might ever need it 24/7. A particularly bad patch in week two depleted our supply.

So we sit, and try not to move. Bowie, bless him, fans us, but he waxes purple in the process, so I tell him to stop. "How're you?" I ask Lola.

"Medium rare."

Why only now, at the end? I wonder. And then this thought is interrupted when the phone rings.

"Hello, this is –"

"Ambassador, it's Hank. The plane got to us in good time. The load-in didn't take as long as we expected, so we're coming your way now."

"That's a problem—the permits are –" I see Lola signaling with more vigor than she's shown to date—"Actually, there are two problems: one, your landing permit isn't valid until four o'clock this afternoon, and two –" Lola has scribbled the word *tarmac* on a scrap of paper—"the runway –"

"Too late, we're already moving."

Bowie antes a "Shit" and I raise him a "Damn," and then Lola goes all in. We ooze toward the vehicle, rounding up the two day guards and telling them to call Issa and Daouda, to announce that they're coming to the airport with us if they want to get paid. We offered American dollars and they unanimously agreed that they preferred cases of water. I asked Washington to put their salary-equivalent on the plane for us. The guards will keep some for family use, but the rest should fetch a small fortune on the black market; it should cover their travel north. Or south. Or west. But *out*.

"Wait," I say.

There's no time for any actual ceremony.

I lower the flag.

Lola helps me fold it, and I tuck it into my tote bag beside the laptop.

We lock the gates. One last time.

Bowie drives. It takes years off my life listening to Adama's poor navigation and Bowie's worse French, but we manage to reach Issa's house, and he (very sensibly) takes the wheel and drives us to Daouda's, where we come to a rolling stop and he piles in. Issa, who used to drive for the French ambassador (and was subsequently fired for stealing water bottles from the car cup holders, so we got him at a bargain-basement rate), has mastered every rut, manhole cover, and pothole along the route. The dust storm has started early; our visibility has gone from "low" to "everything is orange" to "praying without ceasing"—but we are delivered unto the airport. Shaken, but, fortunately, not stirred.

We arrive in time to see the plane touch down, and to watch its wheels lodge in the glutinous asphalt.

Perfect.

There's an abandoned stair car fifty yards down the runway, with the key taped to the wheel; Issa expertly guides it up against the plane.

The pilot, co-pilot Hank, and Hank's crew emerge, just as several men in camouflage approach from the southwest. "Government,"

Lola announces. Everyone pretends they're not relieved. Hank says, "First thing, we need to dig out –"

The government men are waving their two copies of the triplicate form like displaced NASCAR officials: white flag, yellow flag. Final lap. Hazard on the track.

They start to argue that our plane can't be here –

"Attendez," I say, to the officials. "Wait," I say, to Hank and his crew. "We need to pay our guards, and then we can deal with everything else."

Hank and his men fetch some of their shovels to help dig out the wheel.

In short order—and in blatant violation of the Foreign Corrupt Practices Act—we manage to settle our airport dispute with a case of water for each of the officials. Having rendered them contented, we offload the crates for the two day guards, and Issa and Daouda, which they load into the Suburban. I turn to say farewell, but they are making their way back toward the plane, picking up extra spades, plunging them into the liquid tar with gusto.

"Mais –" I begin.

We've settled up –

Daouda turns back and smiles. "Sans problème, Madame."

It is a kindness I cannot begin to repay; the only thing to do is to emulate them. I take off my blazer and fold it, set it down on top of my tote; I take off my hat; I grab a shovel, too.

We do not whistle while we work.

For a few moments, all is digging and silence.

And then there are more men—dozens, hundreds—in camouflage, and they, too, are crying out, and Lola yells, "Take cover!" a split second before a bee whizzes past my ear.

It isn't a bee.

I fling my arm out in an unmistakable gesture to tell the guards to run; they take the Suburban and go with a merry, "Que Dieu vous bénisse!" May God bless us all, really, I think, but Bowie grabs my shoulder, pulling me down ahead of him; we run at a crouch to cower behind the stair car. The guards are unarmed, but Hank and his men apparently aren't; they've scrambled back into the plane for their weapons. I hear them above, shooting, using the plane door as cover.

Lola fells two men without blinking.

And –

"Ma'am." A rasp. A rale.

Bowie.

A red butterfly racing across his chest.

The Department put me in a class on this, just before I left...the instructor said I'm supposed to put plastic over it, to prevent a sucking chest wound. My kingdom for a sterile dressing, or even that duct tape we used on the tarp yesterday. Oh God. Bowie... I've got to say something...it seems hours have passed but it's just nauseating panic; it's surely been only seconds...

"I'm here for you."

I take off my button-down—mercifully I put on an undershirt this morning—and use it as a compress/seal. It's terrible, completely inadequate, but there's nothing else.

"Ma'am..."

"Don't speak," I say, rubbing his forehead. I start calculating how we can possibly get him to a hospital...but now there's bloody froth at his lips, like bubbles in a strawberry soda. Lola ducks behind the stairs with us, takes one look at Bowie, and shakes her head. A spasm rocks my entire body as he coughs, spurting blood—a fountain in the desert.

"Bowie," I whisper. My entire profession is words, and I have none that rise to this occasion, when the only light left in my life is about to go out. "Thank you for your optimism, and your kindness—and your handstands—in an otherwise irredeemable situation."

He makes no answer, but he smiles faintly...

...then doesn't.

"Madame l'Ambassadeur!"

I recognize the voice.

He's been saying Saigneur all along, I realize.

He goes on at some length, very formally, in a three-pronged argument (this, I note, irrelevantly, is one of the more persistent and annoying vestiges of French rule) and notes that we have a) not gotten *his* permission to land at the airport, b) have been giving away the water we promised him, and c) are generally behaving like entitled white colonials.

I can't argue with that last point and won't try, but we did tell him yesterday that we were coming through. And it's not true that we've given away his precious loot—the cases for the embassy guards were a separate allotment, and the ones we gave the airport staff part of our getaway kit. I begin to describe these arrangements—but warlords in every place and clime are not known for paying heed to females. Even a duly accredited envoy of the United States.

The conversation devolves to the point where he calls me a cheat ("Tricheuse!") and I say, "I'm sure we can work something out,"—surely there's booze on the plane?

"Yes," he agrees. His tone puts me in mind of winter mornings in front of the television, the Grinch deciding to relieve the Whos of their moveable property. "My final offer is: anything drinkable on the plane except for the one case I'll leave you...and I'll let *you* go."

Lola looks at me, and I look at Lola.

She shakes her head.

In answer, I pick up my hat.

And put it on her.

Even in the shadow of the stair car, I can see her blanch. "No!" she hisses, even as I pick up my blazer and start slipping it over her shoulders. "Ma'am, this is crazy –"

"It's a calculation," I say. "The options are: you go and I die, I go and you die, we both try to go and, not only do they shoot both of us, they put dozens of bullets or an RPG into the plane, and take down the pilots and Hank's men. Survey says –"

"Ma'am –"

"*Dolores*," I interrupt. "Please call me Sophia. It's been a pleasure serving with you. Now, as your ambassador, I'm ordering you to get on that plane."

How *Casablanca*, I muse, demonstrating that the human mind is ever-capable of inappropriate whimsy. She frowns but slouches into my hat and blazer, and picks up my tote. We embrace, very briefly, very awkwardly, and I say, "Good luck. Please give my notebook to the historian's office."

"I will," she says, offering a funny nod, and—keeping her face carefully turned away from the gunmen—starts up the stair car steps, as three of Hank's men carry down the rest of the beverages and leave them at the bottom. I obediently roll the stairs away from the plane, keeping myself in their bulky trapezoidal shadow, until the silver bird is airborne.

Soon enough, the minions round me up and take me to their leader.

"Vous êtes bien folle, Madame l'Ambassadeur," the Saigneur says, cracking a hard candy between his teeth.

I don't dispute his (not unreasonable) proposition that I am, indeed, crazy.

He places the gun to my temple. "Au revoir," he says. And—*how can it be?—how?*—the ester trailing from his lips conjures a ripe, red strawberry.

The Plover's Egg

Allison Epstein

Allison Epstein lives in Chicago, where she is pursuing her MFA at Northwestern University. Her work has been published in Hypertrophic Literary, the Chicago Reader, the American Book Review, and others. Find her on Twitter @AllisonEpstein2.

The mariner entered the hall with frost in his beard and a woman in his arms. She was wrapped in his wolf-pelt coat and curled against his chest, so I couldn't see her face. But I could see the mariner's, beneath the fringe of his fur cap and tangled brows. The shadow of his beard, his narrow body like an otter's. His arms cradled a tangle of white hair and gray fur. One small fist, tightly balled, rested on his collarbone.

Conversation stopped immediately. The count's other guests—lords, hunters, wealthy men worth flattering with a banquet—were hungry, but they wanted the gossip more. And though I wouldn't have passed up fresh fish if they'd thought to offer me some, I still preferred the story. I stood behind the table, waiting until I was needed, waiting to hear.

"We thought we lost you, Aleksander," one of the hunters said. "You can't wander off, you'll get left behind."

"Though looks like you've got your own catch," said another.

A ripple of laughter followed. The scent of fish rising from the table took on a rotten edge. I swallowed, tasting salt and acid.

The mariner, Aleksander, nodded at the table. "Clear a space."

I knew he meant me. I shifted the platters of salmon aside, and he laid the woman between them. Away from his arms, she was smaller than I supposed. Her face was half-shielded by her white hair, though she could hardly have been older than me. I longed to run my hand through it, see if it was as smooth as it looked.

"Where on earth," said the count from the head of the table, "did you get that?"

Aleksander didn't look away from the woman. With one hand, he brushed a lock of hair from her face. Her cheekbone when revealed stood sharp as a mountain.

"She was under the ice," he said. "I followed tracks to the river, and I saw her hair. Drifting. Like kelp, but brighter. Like she was calling me."

Her pale skin had a lavender tinge. Frostbite, or something further. I reached to tug the coat over the woman's bare feet, which rested near the discarded tail of the salmon.

Aleksander caught me by the wrist. His hand was hot even through his glove. "Don't," he said.

I stepped back but didn't look away. A knife shone beside the platter of fish, and a two-pronged fork plated with gold.

The count and his men speculated about the woman's origins, her purpose, her use. Their suggestions grew wild. A lost noble-woman from Petersburg, a prophet sent by the Lord, a gift from the tsar for the count's loyal service. But Aleksander said nothing more, and the woman said nothing at all.

"Take her," the count said finally. "Let her rest."

The mariner stepped forward, but the count put a hand on his arm.

"Don't be ridiculous. Let Marya take her. That's why we have servants."

Aleksander froze. I wanted to laugh in his face. Instead, I took the woman in my arms. She was easy to lift. His coat smelled of tobacco and lemon, not scents I associated with the sea. The woman leaned her head against my shoulder and left a damp patch on my dress.

The count turned back to the salmon. He pared off a hunk of flesh and placed it on a plate, then gestured with a knife at the mariner. Aleksander's face stiffened. Here was a man who'd had a knife turned on him before, and not in friendship.

"Sit," said the count. "Eat."

The mariner sat. I watched his lips close around the pink flesh, watched him chew. Then I took the woman upstairs, to an empty bedroom where she could rest.

She was damp still, but I wouldn't undress her. I couldn't imagine the fear of it: waking in a strange bed in a strange house, wearing clothes that weren't yours and not knowing what happened to get you into them. Besides, she wasn't shivering, and her breath was regular. I laid her in bed, covered her with blankets and spread the mariner's coat atop them all. Then I lit a fire and sat in the wooden chair beside it. Letting the night pass, watching her.

She looked so small under the thick blankets. This grand chamber, this half-poster bed, this roaring fire, it seemed too big for her, and at the same time too small.

"You can go," Aleksander said from the door.

I hadn't heard him coming. Years of walking on creaking decks must have taught him how to move softly. He sat on the edge of the woman's bed, his hip a hand's-width away. Even across the room, I thought I could feel heat rolling from him.

"I'll stay," I said. "Make sure she's taken care of."

He ignored me. He'd given an order, and I'd follow it, because that's what orders were for. Aleksander's fingers trailed down the woman's leg above the blankets. The woman sighed and leaned into his touch. I pictured his hand falling to the floor, an awkward claw cut off at the wrist.

"Call for me if you need help," I said.

I left her with the mariner and went to bed without eating, without changing clothes, without permission. I lay staring at the ceiling. Directly above me, the woman was sleeping. The outline of her body would mirror mine. I closed my eyes and saw the net of her hair across my pillow, crackling like spiderweb fractures in glass.

The care of the white-haired woman was assigned to me. The count's staff was small, leaving us little choice but to take on tasks that weren't ours. Apparently I could be spared from the laundry easier than the others, a fact I tried not to take as an insult. In any case, I was happy to go. It got me out of the scalding water for a few hours, away from the steam and the tang of lye. And it got me into the woman's room, so I'd be there when she woke.

One day went by, then two. The next morning, when I opened the door, she was sitting up in bed, and the fire was out. She'd found a book somewhere and was reading it, her knees up toward her chest. Eyes on the page, she looked asleep still. It was the only view of her eyelashes I'd ever had. Then she looked up. Her eyes were more gold than brown, almost yellow.

"Good morning," I said. My breath hung thick in front of me.

She set the book aside and gestured for me to sit on the bed. When I did, the scent of lemon seemed to follow.

"Thank you for taking care of me, miss," the woman said.

Those golden eyes, so difficult to meet. "No thanks," I said, "and no miss. Just Marya."

"Elizaveta," the woman said, and touched my shoulder. I couldn't have put into words what exactly made me tremble. But I could meet her eyes now. Beside us, frost clouded the high windows.

"Let me light a fire," I said, after too long a pause. "You must be freezing."

Elizaveta laughed. "Not at all. In fact"—she lifted the wolf-pelt coat from her legs and held it out to me. "Take it. I saw you shiver."

"I couldn't," I said, as I put it over my shoulders. "They'll think it's theft."

She grinned. "It wouldn't be the first coat you've stolen."

No. But that coat had been bearskin, and it smelled of nothing but the back of a wardrobe. My father's coat, taken late at night with his money still in the pocket. Cold through the threadbare elbows as I tapped against Sonya's window, urged her to come and say a proper goodbye. The kind my father threatened to kill me for, the reason I was running. She opened the window, glanced over her shoulder, climbed out into the snow. Sonya's pale brown hair, almost amber. Sonya's nine narrow fingers, the rounded stub of the tenth from a childhood accident with a door. Sonya's last kiss, just above the collar of the bearskin coat. Sonya's breath, thickening around the word *Go*.

I'd left home that night. Run to the count's manor seeking work, and found it. But I hadn't told anyone here why I'd left. And Elizaveta had spoken to no one but me.

I should have denied it. Claimed it all to be a misunderstanding. It wasn't safe admitting it to anyone, certainly not a stranger. Still, I'd heard nothing, no news, in a year.

"Did you know her?"

"She's safe," Elizaveta said. "Her parents sent her away, to Poland, and she married a fisherman's son. Someone should have told you."

How could anyone have? How could anyone know?

Elizaveta laid a hand on my shoulder. I flinched as if from lightning.

"I'm sorry," she said. "I've frightened you."

"No," I said. "Not at all."

I smiled and left her to her book and her business. Through the leaded window in the hall, snow swirled upward and sideways. Like sea spray, fast enough to drown in. It had snowed before, snowed yesterday, snowed all winter, but never like this.

I returned to the laundry, where at least the hot water would keep me safe. By nightfall, the snow had piled eight fresh inches and was only falling faster.

My father told me once about a friend of a cousin, Fyodor Ivanovich, who lived in a village twenty miles from Smolensk. One winter morning, Fyodor came across a young man in the woods, red-haired and black-eyed, and offered him a drink from his flask. The young man smiled with teeth too small and close together. He took a short drink and gave the full flask back empty.

"Strong," he said with a wince.

"That's the idea," Fyodor said. "Enough vodka and you can't feel the cold. You're sure you'll be all right alone, friend?"

The man bowed. "Perfectly. Thank you," he said, "for the hospitality." And with that, he turned off into the woods.

When Fyodor returned home, he saw the woodpile outside his house had doubled in size, and the room was warm, though no fire burned there. Out the window, a set of fox tracks circled the house. No trail led to or away from them. From then on, an etching of a fox hung among the icons of saints in the east corner of Fyodor's home. It stayed there until the day he died.

My father held this story up as a warning against credulity, of how folk religion blinded men to reason. Imagine, he'd say, thinking you owed any sort of reverence to a fox. Now, I thought of the way sunlight rippled off Elizaveta's hair, and I wondered. Pure white and lavender, like scales through water. Those yellow eyes that knew me.

Elizaveta recovered faster than I expected. Soon she moved about the house, receiving a noble's welcome from the count. Still, she called me to her room at night to keep her company. She felt at ease with me, she said. What I felt was nothing at all like ease, but I never thought of refusing. I could have stayed with her forever, basking in her attention.

My conversation wasn't worth her time. The great adventure of my life, my love for Sonya and my escape, could be told in an afternoon. Nothing happened to me here. Stupid gossip from downstairs, who'd insulted whom and why. The banality was why I'd come. Predictability was safe.

But safety wasn't what I wanted now.

When Elizaveta spoke, I'd abandon everything to listen. Sometimes she'd slip into a language I didn't understand. The words were hollow, deep green streaked with light. Sometimes she told me about the currents—cold and then warm—that danced through her hair and around her knees. She spoke of the salmon that nuzzled her toes, and how she suspected she'd once heard them purr. She spoke of the mariner's booted feet overhead. The ice creaking. How in a moment the fish were gone, and then in the next so was she.

She never told me how she'd come to be beneath the ice. Whether she'd fallen from above or drifted from below. What happened during her first breath above, when the mariner pulled her to shore. I didn't dare ask.

I knew from the moment I heard the two of them together. Even from the other end of the hall. No one else heard, but then, no one else was so attuned to her voice. No one needed to know like I did.

The door to Elizaveta's bedroom was closed, but a warm light poured through the cracks around it. It glowed orange-yellow, the beak and talons of some great bird. I stood there watching it dance.

Elizaveta's voice came through the door. The music of it only, not the sense. A laugh. And then a response, in a voice that rolled like waves. The mariner's voice. Aleksander.

The doorknob seared my palm. I dropped my hold on it like a living thing. A fire must have raged inside, warmer than it ever burned for me. For a moment, I saw myself from above: a short, solid, plain girl with a freckled face and servants' clothes, standing outside a locked door. Flushed, I turned my back on their laughter.

But I knew I'd come when she called.

He left gifts for her, small trinkets from his travels. Elizaveta would show them to me when I came after dark. They stood neatly along the mantle, publicly displayed, glittering like trophies. A pocket mirror with a jeweled peacock on the front—Elizaveta never looked at her reflection—a silver locket with a clasp like an oyster—she never wore jewelry.

Once he brought a plover's egg painted with a map of the globe. She showed it to me, brimming with pride. I took it and sat on the end of the bed, turning it over in my hands. It was beautiful. I couldn't fight that. Soft blues and sea greens, done with a brush no wider than a grain of rice. Each country was there, though warped slightly to suit the oblong shape. I ran the lines of my palms along loving, minute renditions of Prussia, Lapland, Persia.

"Look," she said, and tapped her fingernail against the shell.

Where her nail had touched, a tiny sea monster snaked through the water beyond Japan.

"Isn't it lovely?" she said.

It was such a little thing. Delicate. And my hands were strong. My knuckles twitched.

Elizaveta snatched the egg from my hands. I'd seen her passionate before, but never angry.

"Find Aleksander," she said. "I want to thank him."

I stood. She tucked the egg under her pillow and waited. I went.

I thought of it all night. The two of them together, tangled, one, sharing the minute world beneath her pillow. I lay alone and hoped the egg would crack.

The next night, when she turned her back on me, I reached one hand beneath the pillow. The egg was still there, unharmed.

I sat on the window-ledge, watching Elizaveta watch me. They'd given her finer clothes, but she sat on the end of the bed with the mariner's old fur coat over her lap. It made her look like an invalid, a young woman trapped in the body of someone much older. The fire had long since burned out. Her yellow eyes shone like glowworms in the dark.

Neither of us had spoken for some minutes. Through the glass, the snow beat encouragement against my back. *Ask her. Ask.*

"Have you ever been in love?" I said.

"Twice."

"With who?"

She shrugged. "I think I loved the salmon."

"And the other time?"

Elizaveta said nothing.

The snow tapped harder against my spine. There was nothing else for it. She hadn't asked for my secret, but she hadn't told me not to share it. And if I didn't, he would. I stood up.

"I've loved twice too," I said.

"Sonya, for the first," she said. "And the other?"

I sat beside her. Moved the coat aside, so the curve of her thighs showed through her wool skirt. "Can I?" I said.

She nodded and then, permission aside, she kissed me.

Poets talk about the heat of love. The sweat between skin and skin, the cloud of a lover's breath on your cheek. They never say anything about the cold.

Elizaveta tasted of salt, of mint, of vodka just shy of frozen. Her hair was soft beneath my hands, softer than I expected. It seemed impossible she would want me, a plain woman with nothing. But when she touched me I forgot it. She wanted me. Her hands, mouth, knees, hips, they all wanted me, and I let them have me, with a shudder of surrender and victory I let them. At the peak my breath spilled from me in a haze that hung there, almost solid, improbable.

I sank back trembling against the bed. Her laugh rang like falling water. When I woke, her bare arm was around my shoulder, and the sheets crackled with frost. I kissed her cold brow and left her. Walking to the laundry through the deserted house, I allowed myself a broad, unshielded smile.

I was elbow-deep in lye and other people's stockings when Aleksander came to me. He sat on the table I used for folding. From the floor, where I knelt over the washtub, he seemed as tall as three men. His legs in their cracked sealskin breeches were spread wide. Each time he crossed my path I saw him more clearly. I thought of him as a cheap magician, revealing his own appearance at will and in pieces. I hadn't noticed the color of his eyes before, their bright salt gray. I hadn't noticed their light, like they'd be kind if someone gave them permission. I hadn't noticed the bite of vodka, which I could smell over the lye.

He wanted something, that was clear. But what did it matter now?

I gestured at his breeches, flicking gray water in his direction. "I'm afraid those are beyond my help."

Aleksander's laugh erased some of the lines from his face. He could be charming. He *was* charming. His hands had pulled Elizaveta from the ice.

"No," he said, "I don't need washing. Sailor's curse. I'll die smelling of the sea."

Now that was a thought.

"You're close with Elizaveta," he said.

The chill of salt on my lips. Her fingers, confident and insistent, frigid yet tender. I almost pitied him, but what I felt couldn't be called pity.

"You could say that."

"I wanted to ask you a favor." Aleksander leaned forward. His eyes were sharper now. "The harbor is frozen, and my ship can't leave."

"Should I end the winter?"

He laughed, though there was nothing in it. "If you could. Otherwise, I'll sail with the thaw. And I want Elizaveta to come with me, as my wife."

The shirt in my hands caught against the washboard. I tugged, but it wouldn't come free. Aleksander reached one callused hand and pulled softly, down. A buttonhole had wrapped around the bottom peg of the board. He could see it clearer from his position. I snatched the shirt away and tossed it over a chair. I would finish it later.

"I don't see what that has to do with me."

"You could tell her, Marya. Convince her. Tell her no one loves her like I do."

He loved her. Aleksander. He'd seen her first through a mirror of ice. Crept in at night, that tall handsome man, trailing a cloud of tobacco and lemon. How did he see her? A prize the water held for him? I could have drowned him in the washtub. I thought of it, his sodden smile, his eyes stinging with lye.

His eyes, no longer so kind. The cruelty of a man with the upper hand.

"Yes," I said, and turned back to the washtub. "I'll tell her."

Leaving the laundry for supper, I saw a thick swirl of frost along the lower windows, one that hadn't been there in the colder hours of the morning. A neat script curled through each pane as if from the tip of a finger.

Marya, Marya, Marya.

On the grounds, visible through the lettering, a woman with white hair walked beside a man. She turned to face him, rose on tiptoe, and brought his face down for a kiss. Her laugh rose in frozen steam. But when I blinked, there was no one there, only my own name.

I didn't tell her. But then, he didn't need help. He only wanted me to know.

Aleksander should have told someone about me. Removed me from the scene. Perhaps he feared Elizaveta would be punished for my actions, I don't know. What I do know is that he told no one, because when the news reached us downstairs, no one thought to lower their voices around me.

The wedding, the other women said, giddy as seagulls. A

wedding in spring, the first day there would be pure sun. The engagement ball first and then, at snowmelt, the wedding.

"Whose wedding?" I asked.

"The mariner's," they said. "Aleksander, that handsome sailor. And the strange woman from the ice."

I saw his eyes as he'd watched me in the laundry. Those kind eyes, those mocking eyes. Those eyes that sparkled like gray water and said to me, *You've lost.*

But I hadn't. Not yet.

"You can't love him," I said.

Elizaveta shrugged, which made pinning on her sleeve that much harder. "Why not?"

We only had half an hour, and I still couldn't get the dress to come together properly. It was a delicate thing, white lace done in tiny scalloped pieces, more like scales than fabric. The intricacy made it impossible to get at the proper seams. This was why I usually washed clothes instead of helping ladies into them. But she'd asked for me. As she shifted her weight, the lace rippled, revealing shades of white I'd never seen before.

"It's not right," I said.

She turned, stopping my work. "What if that's why I like him?"

My palms itched, but I pressed them against my thigh. She hadn't said *love.*

"What other wrong things do you like?" I said.

Elizaveta took the one sleeve I'd half-pinned to her shoulder and tugged it off. It hung in her hand like a dead thing before she tossed it away, into the hearth. There hadn't been a fire there in days, not since Aleksander's last visit, but I hadn't swept the ashes either. The scales turned gray as a cloud of cinders rose around them.

"Let's leave the dress like this," she said.

I stepped back and looked. Lace brushed her collarbone, slumped down the curve of her shoulders. The fabric moved as she breathed, rippling in and out, frayed.

I reached into my pocket and took out a strand of beads threaded onto a string. I'd taken them from my prayer rope, silver beads with a single yellow one at the center. I tied the ends of the string around her wrist. She held it toward the candlelight, catching sparks in the beads.

"It's lovely," she said.

I kissed the back of her hand. "You'll be late."

The slate-gray hall had been transformed for the occasion. High-ceilinged and vast, it felt intimate, every flat surface holding candles ensconced in crystal, vases with bursts of purple hyacinths and yellow crocuses. The light fluttered with each brush of skirt, each breath.

And there, at the center, they danced.

I watched them from the door. She in lace alive and breathing in the glow. He in black, his hair slicked smooth and glistening. One hand softly holding hers, the other around her waist. A single crocus behind her ear with the stem tucked into her braid. I couldn't dance, had never learned the steps, but anyone could see the grace that moved between them like a living thing. My beads glittered against his shoulder. His fingers curled into her hair, and they stood still in the center of a whirling room as he kissed her.

"Excuse me." A boy stood behind me with a tray of aqua vitae to resupply the high table. I was blocking his way.

"Thank you." I took two glasses and moved aside. By the time I turned, Elizaveta and Aleksander had rejoined the dance.

The drink was powerful. I felt frozen and flaming, wild as the snow against the window. I wandered the halls, through corridors I had no business being in, with a detour back to the hall for another round of aqua vitae. When I woke the next morning, it was in a third-floor alcove, with a sharp headache and no clear memory of how I'd come there. I dragged myself to the privy to vomit and then stumbled to my own bed.

The next time I woke it was well past noon, and a single crocus petal rested beside my cheek on the pillow. Pale yellow, almost white, narrow at the top and widening to a curve. No larger than my thumb.

It wasn't a promise, nor was it an apology.

What I took it for was permission.

Most evenings, I knew, Elizaveta retreated to a private place to pray. It wasn't her bedroom—she hadn't hung any icons along the wall—and it wasn't the church—I'd have seen her there—but it was somewhere. Aleksander wasn't a praying man, but he was predictable. When Elizaveta went off, he'd retreat to his own temple: the stables. He was a horseman through and through, everyone knew it. Perhaps he felt their movement was as close to the sea as he could get here.

It wasn't, which I meant to show him.

I'd grown up on the banks of the Neva. Tugged fish from it in summer, known which patches of ice would hold my weight in winter. I'd followed it from my father's house to here, tracing its undulations like a sea monster lain flat. I knew which bends were rocky, which stretches unexpectedly deep. The mariner knew the sea, but the river was mine.

Aleksander was where I'd expected him. He occupied himself with the care of a white gelding, ingratiating himself with the woody musk of its smell. The horse nuzzled its nose into his shoulder as he stroked its coat. Perfectly at its ease. I hated how animals trusted him.

"I hope you enjoyed yourself last night," Aleksander said as he turned to me.

An insult, but that didn't matter. "Elizaveta sent me," I said. "She has something to show you. A wedding present."

He patted the gelding's neck and leaned against the stall door. There was a lopsided confidence to him, one that would rock and adapt to the tides. A belief that what he received from the world was his due. He could have had anyone he wanted without effort.

"She doesn't have to do that," he said.

"And yet," I said. "I'll take you to her."

We left the stables at dusk. By the time we passed the edge of the grounds and entered the woods, it was fully dark. The moon hung bright, nearly full, but shaded by the bare branches interlaced above us. There were no human footprints here but Aleksander's and mine. Just elongated tracks of rabbits, a few smaller pads from voles or stoats. I heard small wings flutter between the trees, but when I raised my head the bird was gone.

"Where is she?" Aleksander's voice fell echoless, swallowed by snow.

Beside me, a thick elm stood with gouges down its bark, evidence of years-old bear claws. I ran my palm along the deepest of them. A splinter tugged my skin though it didn't stick. My father's fur coat brushed my chin. The glow of distant manor lights. A home behind, something else ahead. How long had it been, since I first came this way in reverse?

"Not far," I said.

Half a mile further, the Neva cut a clearing through the woods. And there, somehow, was Elizaveta.

She dangled her legs in the water, swirling her ankles in small loops. Ripples overlapped, this way and that. Around her, as I'd known it would, the river shone with deceptive ice that wouldn't hold a person's weight. I wanted to melt away. Bead into glittering drops that fell to earth, leaving a soft hollow in the snow.

"This was beneath you," she said.

Nothing was beneath me. She should have known that.

"A dirty trick," she said, and pulled her bare calves from the river. "I expected more." She folded her legs, pale skin directly against the snow. My flesh prickled in sympathy, but hers didn't redden. Her purple veins stuck out like paint-strokes.

Aleksander's eyes widened. He wasn't stupid. The river here, fast and deep. A body pressed against the bottom of the ice with palms splayed out. How close he'd come to his death. Saved by my own lie coming true despite myself. I saw something harden behind his eyes. A door had shut that couldn't be opened.

"Come with me," he said, and grabbed Elizaveta's wrist. "Leave her."

He pulled her to her feet so sharply I winced. Her bare feet left skids in the snow before she righted herself.

She looked down. Her skin glowed paler around Aleksander's fingers. "Let go," she said.

"You knew," he said. "The two of you, against me. I should have known." His other hand reached, grasping for her hair.

Elizaveta didn't fight him. One minute he yanked her head back to expose her throat, and the next she stood alone two feet away from him. She took a step toward the river. She shook her head.

"I hoped for better from you, too," she said.

Aleksander started to speak. But he didn't make it far. Even the river slowed down to watch.

It started slowly. A shivering of her silhouette, a rough slickness rising where before there had been cool unbroken skin. Speckles dotted her brow and shoulders. Her pale hair gathered up and back into a mesh-like fin. A quiet breath, like the *thwack* of snow falling from a roof. The lavender tinge like veins running shallowly beneath scales.

The eyes shifted last. The pupils widened, but the yellow irises remained. Scornful. I saw those eyes looking at me from a wall of painted icons framed in gold. Demanding more from me, better than what I'd given.

The salmon twisted its tail mid-fall and arced headfirst into the black waters of the Neva. Ripples spread in perfect circles, striking the banks. The wind twisted, and snow caught in my lashes. I tasted mint, cold enough to ache.

On the riverbank, a perfect circle had melted from the snow. The plover's egg rested in the center as if laid by a careful mother. It stood with the narrow end pointed toward the stars. If I dusted it with snow, I'd still see her fingerprints on it.

Twisted around the base of the egg was a strand of silver beads.

The ripples faded, and then the Neva was still.

Aleksander moaned. I knew the sound as if my heart had made it. He sank to his knees. I sat beside him, past the point of being cold. The snow quickened to a rapid burial. Flakes nestled in the mariner's tangled brows, in the brim of his fur cap. Too harsh to walk. The manor was impossibly far, and the cold sat hard in my bones. No one would come this way, not this long after sundown.

I looked over my shoulder, but I couldn't see the way home. All I saw were three figures in the snow, glittering and transient, dancing on curls of wind into the dark.

Violent Silence

Elizabeth Guilt

Elizabeth Guilt reads and writes short stories to make her daily commute on the London Underground more enjoyable.

"This is Sherri." I look up. "Sherri, this is Officer Garth."

Sherri and I shake hands. Her hand is steady and grips mine with just the right degree of firmness. Her fingers are cool, and it feels like she is wearing a latex glove.

She looks me straight in the eye. Is that contempt? Hostility? I'm not sure. With the old ones you could always tell; their range of expressions was limited—and documented in the manuals if you had any doubts.

My boss, having introduced us, runs through the details as if we didn't know already. This is to be a field test of Sherri's abilities. She is in command, and I am to follow her instructions unless I feel it is unsafe to do so. If I feel the need to take charge, the experiment will be deemed a failure.

We both nod. Then we pick up our packs, and head out to the jeep. Instinctively, I walk towards the driver's door but Sherri pulls me up.

"I'll drive, Garth. The details for the route are in the door pocket."

That tells me a couple of things. Firstly, she doesn't have the route memory or mapping abilities of the custom driving droids;

she still needs a navigator. Secondly, her motor control is good enough to drive the heavy, old-fashioned jeep.

I get the kit out of the pocket and start flicking switches, making sure the radar's reports correlate with what I can see out of the windows. There's a stretch of main road before I need to start giving directions, and I steal a couple of glances at Sherri.

From a distance, you'd definitely mistake her for human. It's not just the shape of her moulded body, her movements are fluid and lifelike.

From a couple of feet away, her skin has the unnatural gloss of polysilicone. Her hair is cut short but I can't tell what it's made from without peering closer. I smile to myself as I realize my mistake: of course her hair isn't cut short. It's just...short. It never grew, never needed cutting.

It's always been difficult not to think of the droids as living beings, even the really dumb, monofunctional ones that were only roughly humanoid.

"Garth?"

"Oh, sorry. Another mile and a half. Then we're taking the track off to the left, just after a stretch of woods."

The journey is reasonably short, and uneventful. I issue directions, matching the scratchy screen to the landmarks. She follows them. We don't attempt any kind of conversation.

Once we're there, Sherri selects the locations for the shelterpods and leaves me to erect them while she fills in the logs. She directs the placing of the radio mast, and briefly outlines where she thinks trouble might come from. I wonder, as I snap up the plastic lashes on the radio mast, who they'd believe if I reported that her decisions were terrible. With a few quiet acts of sabotage, I could make her seem unfit for command, and shut down the whole program that created her.

I pause for a moment, staring into the distance. I don't want to believe that they can create a consciousness flexible enough, general-skilled enough, to take command. I want to think that I—a human—am still somehow better than the tireless, perfectly-skilled droids coming from the factories out east. But at the same time, rejecting Sherri means dooming another generation of humans to fight and die on these wastelands. I need to accept that the machines can take this over.

Back in camp I heat my rations up and, once I've eaten them, build a fire. The halostove is now such old tech that it looks antique, and yet humans still build fires whenever they camp. I don't need it—and Sherri certainly doesn't—but it gives us something to do, and something to fiddle with, and something to sit round. No one ever swilled beer or talked crap around a halostove.

We discuss a few details of the program for tomorrow. They want observations of one of the closer rebel camps; observations from up close, and a list of details we need to fill in. I figure I might as well play my role as the rookie under command, and I ask my question with wide eyes.

"Is this going to be dangerous, Sherri?"

"Yes," she nods. "That's why they're trying to build droids to do it, Garth."

"Fair point." I shut up.

***

The mission goes off as planned. Sherri directs it perfectly, and way before the sun begins to set we're home and dry, broadcasting the pictures back to base. Now that I'm starting to feel that she can be trusted, I'm relaxing into the role of junior and kind of enjoying passing the responsibility for once. I have to make an extra report on her progress, and I deliberately move out of earshot before I begin talking into the receiver.

By the time I've finished, Sherri's rebuilt the fire and set a ration pack on the halostove.

"Are those for me?"

Apparently this model of droid has enough facial animation to raise an eyebrow at me. She shrugs, too.

"To be honest, the fire is as much for me as it is for you, Garth."

"Yes?" I grab my rations and tuck in. But I'm curious. "What do you get from the fire? Warmth?"

She shrugs again. "Not really. I can hold my hands out and feel that it's hot, but it's not pleasurable, it's just temperature data. I can watch the flames dance, though, and look for pictures in the fire, and know that it'll keep the darkness away."

I realize that my mouth is open, and close it. Language circuitry appears to have come on a hell of a lot in the past six months.

"Besides," she continues, "I have a lot of happy memories of sitting round fires."

"They created you with memories?"

Sherri looks at me quizzically. "They...I guess they didn't tell you how they created me, then."

"Just that you were an upgrade, designed to be more of an all-rounder."

"Typical."

She falls silent, but I'm used to that from droids. They run up against the end of their programming, and just stop mid-conversation. Then I look at her face again in the firelight and see that she's uncomfortable. As if she's trying to work out what to say.

"Should I ask?"

She shakes her head. "No one ever mentioned it was supposed to be a secret. My body's the same as the regular high-end droids, but I'm not programmed." She taps her head. "One bit's organic."

"What? Who?"

"Officer Sherri Latimer. Died at 27. A motorbike accident, they tell me. About two years ago. I'm basically a brain in a really fancy jar."

It takes me a moment to take that in. "And you have her memories?"

"My memories. Yes. I've commanded hundreds of missions like this before, but now we have to check that I still can."

I try briefly to imagine how it must be to find yourself transported into a plastic shell of a body, your brain wired in to allow you to command it to move, to walk, to poke the fire. I can't quite grasp the idea.

"How is it?"

"It's better than the alternative."

***

I don't sleep all that well, tossing and turning in my shelterpod as I think about Officer Sherri Latimer. She is, surely, a human regardless of what her body is made from. And yet these are the "machines" who are supposed to be saving us from enemy bullets.

It feels impolite to ask. But eventually, as we are making our way to a different rebel camp the following morning, I bring it up.

She laughs, apparently without bitterness.

"It takes fairly serious damage to stop me from moving. I could probably get back to camp. Even if my head is completely severed, the systems will keep my brain alive for around five days. Transmitters should help people find me and then they just have to stick a new body on. It's not perfect, but it's a hell of a lot better chance than you would stand."

We chat as we walk cautiously along. It's strange to talk to a droid without having to pick my words, without having to think through whether my sentence is logical or contains metaphors too abstract for them to process. I think that I would have liked Officer Latimer, if I'd met her.

She is mid-anecdote about a tour of duty in the mountains when the screaming sound of seeker bullets tears past us. I hit the deck, and Sherri lands on top of me, spreading her body over mine.

"I give out less infrared than you," she whispers. "Stay still."

She's lighter than I expect, lighter than an adult woman. I hold my breath, hoping she's enough of a shield to keep the bullets off. We hear them ditch harmlessly a short distance away, then there is worse news: voices.

Our eyes meet. Technically I should wait for her order, but we nod at each other as we mouth the same word.

"Run."

There are shots behind me as I sprint through the trees. Just regular shots; seekers are expensive, and they now know where we are. I think I can hear Sherri's footsteps behind me, though the sound of my own blood pounding in my ears soon drowns out most other things.

I twist back down the narrow pass, and eventually manage to snatch a glance over my shoulder. Sherri is keeping up, and there is no sign of pursuit. I spot a slim crack in the rock face, a narrow cave, and dive into it. I head back into the shadows, and collapse. Sherri drops silently next to me, not even out of breath. In the quiet of the cave, I feel the thunder of my breathing echoing and try to get it under control.

Ten minutes or so later, Sherri creeps to the cave mouth and peers out. She's gone for a few minutes, then she's back.

"It's clear. We need to get back to the camp." She maps out a route, taking advantage of what cover there is, and taking in a high point that will give us a good view of whether anyone is following. Our approach will let us see if there is anyone skulking in our camp. It's the perfect decision.

We move swiftly, but the route is circuitous and it's already dark before we're back. We make our reports straight away, giving locations and times and our very limited guesses at numbers.

"You sort your food out, Garth, I'll set up the perimeter alarms. Oh, and no fire tonight."

Again, Sherri's commands are exactly in line with what I'd do.

I heat up my rations as quickly as I can, then pack the halostove away. She joins me, sitting and looking at the place the fire would have been, but she doesn't say anything.

Without the fire, it gets cold sitting in the darkness. We haven't discussed the attack at all, beyond the banal stats we sent back to base, and I feel as if there is something on Sherri's mind.

"I'm going to go and hole up in my shelter. If you want to talk, you're welcome to come and sit inside."

She looks at me, with another ambiguous expression, but still says nothing.

Fifteen minutes later, I'm all wrapped up for sleeping when I hear her voice. "Can I come in?"

"Sure."

The shelterpods are designed for one, but they're just about roomy enough for company. Sherri squeezes in and sits with her arms wrapped tightly around her legs.

"Are you cold?"

She shakes her head. "I don't get cold. Although I can tell you it's about eleven and a half degrees out there."

She pauses for a long time, and I wonder if she feels responsible for the attack, for my safety.

"All your decisions today were right, Sherri. You couldn't have known we'd get shot at."

"I know." She sounds a little offended. Of course; I'm speaking to someone with as much operational experience as I have myself.

"I'm sorry, that was patronizing."

She closes her eyes. "Don't worry about it"

"But something's wrong, isn't it?"

Sherri rubs her hands over her face. It's a very natural gesture, and I wince as I hear the squeak of her fingers against her plastic cheeks. So does she.

"That's one of the few noises my body makes."

"What?"

She rubs her hands together, and there is a long-drawn creaking noise. "Stupid isn't it? My stomach doesn't rumble. My joints don't crack. I don't cough, or sneeze, or fart. But my skin makes a noise."

I'm not sure what to say, and it probably shows on my face.

"It's a stupid thing, Garth, but I miss the noise. Humans are never silent. Think of running away today. When we stopped in the cave your heart was pounding, you were breathing heavily. I could practically hear your blood moving through your veins."

"I don't breathe. I don't have a pulse. When I stop there is nothing to show I was even running. No adrenaline, no fight for breath. Just a violent silence where the drum of my heartbeat should be."

Her head and shoulders droop. I guess whatever lubricates her eyes is no use for expressing how she feels.

"Feedback for the engineers?" I suggest. It's hardly consolation, but all my life I've been trained to solve problems, and I've nothing else to offer.

She shakes her head. "They're not interested. They've made me as efficient as possible. Any mechanism that disrupts that is off the table. They gave me a soundloop for when I lie down at night, but it's just white noise. It's not the same."

I shuffle in my sleeping gear, suddenly aware of the sound of my own breath, of my rations gurgling through my gut, of the organic echo in my ears as I swallow. Without even thinking about it, I hold out my arms, inviting Sherri to lie down with me.

She hesitates for a moment, clearly uncertain what I'm asking. Even I'm not entirely sure.

Then, slowly, she moves across the shelter and lies down with her head on my chest. She's still strangely light, and through the thermal layers I can't feel how cool her body is. I wrap my arms around her.

I breathe deeply, feeling my lungs inflate and the sound rattle round in my chest. She nods once or twice in time with my heartbeat and smiles a little as she powers down.

Blue Lips and Frozen Lashes

Alexandra Grunberg

Alexandra Grunberg is a Glasgow-
based author, poet, and screenwriter.
Her short stories have appeared in
various online magazines including
Daily Science Fiction, Fantastic
Stories of the Imagination, and Flash
Fiction Online. She is the resident
screenwriter for the film production
company Magic Dog Productions.

The girl looked too small to be hiking on her own.

Beitris knew that many children started hillwalking early, exploring the dips and peaks of the Cairngorms and the Trossachs in small packs, acting as their own guardians. But this girl was alone, not in a pack, not surrounded by the whoops and hollers that meant safety as much as entertainment. And though she may have found her way back to the path if this were Arthur's Seat or Ben A'an, Ben Nevis was hardly a hill.

"Hello?" called Beitris.

The little girl did not respond. She hugged her body, hugged her puffy coat. One of her gloves was missing.

Children could hike Ben Nevis. But not alone. And not during the winter.

The girl was a little way off the path. Beitris slid down to her. She saw the flash of a bright pink hat as the girl's head shot up when Beitris skid on some loose icy stones, but the girl did not know where to look with her eyes squeezed shut. Her eyelashes were white with frost, and Beitris wondered if they had frozen together.

"Let's get you back to the path."

Beitris put her hand on the girl's shoulder. The girl did not respond, but she did move. She trembled, the movement shaking flakes of snow from her shoulders. Beitris realized it had begun to snow again, and she frowned at the sky. She would be fine, she knew her way all over Ben Nevis, but no parents should have taken their daughter hiking on the mountain if it was going to snow. The snow covered the gorges, making cliffs look like easy shortcuts, and there was no time to scream before the light powder layer gave way to empty air.

Beitris stopped at the edge of the path. The new layer of snow was masking any sign of past travelers, any clue as to whether people had marched up the path abandoning their slow ward, or if they were down below, waiting, fretting. Beitris grabbed the girl's hand.

It felt like ice.

She looked at the fingers interlacing with hers, and they were already pale blue, and where they gripped her, pure white. Her hair was the same white now, dusted snow white, and her lips matched the blue tint of her hand. She could have been an ice princess. Beitris shivered, though she was used to the weather. This girl could have been a little fairy, and it was not unbelievable, not up here. Not when the snow danced as it fell, whirling in tight circles and then breaking into pairs, hugging trees and ground and eyelashes and melting against skin like the softest kiss. But not melting against skin so cold. There, it clung, desperate, needy. There, it waited, patient, for the skin to lose all heat and turn to ice.

Beitris shook her head. This girl was not an ice princess, not a fairy. She was a lost daughter and she needed to return home.

It felt wrong to go down when she was so near the top, so near that sense of accomplishment, but she was sure that the girl's parents were waiting below, that their child had run past them, and that they had not abandoned her. Beitris had seen other children run wild on the path, run up, up, up towards the top, and she understood the urge. She guided the little girl down the path, holding her hand steady, guiding with her other hand on the back of the puffy coat. Soon there were panicked voices, yelling at each other, like that would help, like that would bring their daughter back any faster.

The little girl gasped, her head turning towards the voices, and now her hand was not so cold. Now the snow did not grip her so forcefully. She eased out of Beitris's grasp, and her fingers were no longer tinged blue, and the ice on her lashes was starting to melt, and she found her voice and began to cry as she ran to her parents.

Beitris let her go. It was right, but it still hurt. She reached out an icy cold hand, and watched the snow dance around her palm, and thanked Ben Nevis, even if she did not accept the gift. It would have taken only a few more minutes for the mountain to claim the child for Beitris, but the girl just looked too small to be hiking on her own. She had a family that wanted her, needed her.

And Beitris had her own family waiting for her at the top of the mountain. She had her own children that she graciously accepted, those boys and girls who whooped and hollered their way to her, unwatched, left alone, and alone meant unwanted, and unwanted meant hers. They may have acted wild, but they needed a guardian. She was happy to guard them; every ice prince and princess that came to her, every person who fell through the deceiving powder of snow without a cry, every child that ran up the mountain and never found their way back down.

Pocketful of Souls

Jennifer Lee Rossman

Jennifer Lee Rossman is an incurable science fiction geek. Her work has been featured in several anthologies and her time travel novella Anachronism is now available from Kristell Ink, an imprint of Grimbold Books. She blogs at jenniferleerossman.blogspot. com and tweets @JenLRossman

Every demon had its own signature look, painstakingly crafted to strike fear into the hearts of mortals.

Anzu took the form of an enormous, fire-breathing bird. Moloch went for the classic "horns and an unnerving number of eyes" aesthetic. Tuchulcha, a chthonic demon who terrorized those darn Etruscans, had hair made of snakes, pointed ears, and the sharp beak of a vulture.

And then there was Amy.

Amy was not like the other demons. While they had been fated to serve the Darkness as punishment—or, to hear the Darkness tell it, reward—for lives filled with unspeakably heinous acts, Amy was a mere child.

No one was quite sure how her pure soul had been bound to the Darkness. Some called it a clerical error, others claimed she had been the cursed result of the union between a human and a demon. Whatever the cause, she had been touched by the Darkness now and the Light could no longer see her, so in the Darkness she remained. And every one of the Darkness's children had to earn their keep.

Amy's chosen form had none of the drama and terror of the

others. She drew upon her appearance in life, giving herself big, blue eyes and a mop of strawberry blonde curls. Her dress and pinafore were reminiscent of Alice, her favorite storybook character, and she wore a perfect, pink bow in her hair, its ribbon matching those on her Easter basket.

"What is the basket for?" the Darkness asked.

Amy grinned, her voice trembling from her barely-contained fit of giggles. "It's where I'm going to put all of the souls!"

***

Amy could barely read, so another demon had to draw up her contract. Other than that, she worked alone, appearing lost and on the verge of tears before desperate people all across the globe.

"I can't find my mommy," she would say, hooking a finger in her mouth and looking up at them with watery eyes that would shame any anime character. Oh, she wouldn't always say it in English. No, the Darkness translated for her, winding around the language center of her brain and rewiring her neurons so she could speak any language.

She said it tickled.

No one could resist Amy. Even the most devious murderer would find themselves stopping in their tracks, drawn to her. Invariably, they would take her hand when she offered it, and that contact was all she needed.

Time froze around them, bird wings stopped mid-flap and peoples' faces contorted as they paused in the middle of a word. The rest of the world slowly shrank away, leaving only Amy and her prospective victim.

She smiled, wiping away the tears. "You've been naughty, haven't you?"

The victim—sometimes a woman, but more often than not a man—stammered. But she knew what he was thinking.

"How could a little girl know what you've done when even the police haven't?" She shrugged. "People tell me I'm precocious, but I dunno what that means."

And then, while they were stunned by the impossible depths of her dimples, she rolled out the contract, her name already signed at the bottom in pink crayon.

"You have been a very bad man," she told him, shaking her finger in imitation of adults. "Someday, you will die, and your soul will go to H-E-L-L." Amy may have been a demon, but that didn't mean she was allowed to swear. "You don't want your soul to go there, do you?"

He shook his head, eyes wide with fear.

"Well, then maybe you should sell it to me. You'll still go to H-E-L-L when you die, but you'll do chores for us instead of being tortured."

Amy couldn't quite pronounce "corrupt the heathens to help bring about Armageddon," so she called it "chores" instead.

The man signed. They always signed, even the most devout believers in their faith, because they knew they would never be able to earn forgiveness from the Light, even through a lifetime of penance. If only they knew the Light didn't particularly care for penance and that its forgiveness could easily be bought with a good loaf of banana bread, the Darkness would have been very lonely indeed; but that particular revelation had never made it into the holy books, and so Amy's latest victim sold his soul like all the others.

Amy put the soul in her basket and started up time again. She liked to make the souls look like chocolates; sometimes, when the Darkness wasn't looking, she would nibble on them a bit.

***

The Darkness had too many souls. It knew this for a fact, because it counted them every day. Couldn't have the Light accusing it of stealing any, not after that incident with the unbaptized babies. (The Darkness couldn't help if one of its demons had misread her own holy book and taken it upon herself to start a heathen nursery.)

And the numbers were definitely off. Not by one or two, which could be explained by the same processing error that made the odd soul go missing, but by hundreds.

The extraneous souls were hardly perfect. If the Light came looking for them, it could be argued that all of their little transgressions added up and that they truly belonged down there. The Darkness certainly had enough lawyers to argue that case. But the Darkness generally favored the deeply evil humans, having no real need for litterbugs and people who recorded Yankees games without the express written permission of Major League Baseball.

A quick check of the Darkness's computer—which, being in Hell, naturally ran Windows Vista—revealed that all of the wayward souls had appeared since the arrival of one demon.

The Darkness looked over the top of the monitor. If it had possessed eyes, it would have narrowed them.

Amy sat on a blackened island amid the lava that made up the floor, humming to herself and playing with dolls.

Dolls which the Darkness did not remember giving her.

Perhaps this Amy child belonged with the Darkness after all, if she was so devious as to turn souls into playthings.

***

Amy approached the man as she always did, doing her best to play the part of a lost, little girl. She'd even rubbed some dirt on her dress to really sell the illusion.

"Mister?" she said quietly. English this time; she didn't want the Darkness tagging along on this trip.

The man turned around, stopping in his tracks when his gaze fell upon the little girl. "Oh. Hello."

"I can't find my mommy," Amy said, extending her hand. But he didn't reach for it, choosing instead to swivel on the spot, searching the busy streets of London.

"Oh dear. What does she look like, sweetheart?"

Amy couldn't touch him. He had to initiate; that was the rule. "She's tall," she said, making her voice sound even younger than she looked. "Real tall, with pointy shoes and yellow hair. Please, Mister. I'm afwaid."

No adult could resist the cutesy "W instead of R" trick. That was how she'd nabbed Jack the Wipper's soul.

The man bent to her level, his face all soft and sad. She let a single tear fall down her cheek, and saw the exact moment his heart broke.

"Oh, you poor thing!" The instant his hand touched hers, the bustling pedestrian traffic halted, and the man gasped at the utter lack of movement and sound. "What is this?" he whispered.

Amy dropped the cute act in favor of a more business-like attitude. She was still a five-year-old girl with enormous eyes and dimples for days, of course, so the effect was negligible. But she pronounced all of her Rs.

"I know what happened," she said, breaking from her usual script. "With your husband."

Grief replaced the man's terror, and he put his hand to his heart. "It was an accident. I got angry when he told me, but I didn't mean to—

"I know," she assured him. "And more importantly, the Darkness knows."

"The...Darkness?"

"Some people call it Hades, or Lucifer...I call it Dar-Dar when we're being silly." Amy shrugged. "But that's not important. Someday, you're going to die, and the Light is going to take you to Heaven unless you give me your soul."

The urgency of her voice confused the man. "Why would I want to give you my soul, if I'm supposed to go to Heaven?"

Her answer was simple. "Because he isn't there."

Amy rolled out the contract. It was messy and misspelled, not to mention written on the back of an envelope, but she hadn't dare let another demon help her with this one.

The man signed it without a second thought, and time started up again as Amy took the man's soul. She turned it not into a chocolate but rather a little doll, and tucked it into her pocket.

* * *

Later that night, when all the other demons were asleep or doing chores, Amy crawled out of bed and took out the box she hid behind a pile of brimstone. Hundreds of teeny dolls smiled up at her blankly, each one holding another doll's hand. Some were enveloped in a great group hug.

Only one lacked companionship. Amy took him out, and pulled the newest one from her pocket. Their painted-on smiles never changed, but she could feel them see each other for the first time.

Under her breath, so the Darkness couldn't hear, Amy gave them voices.

"I missed you so much!"

"Me too. What are you doing here? I hope you didn't sell your soul."

"I did, but I won't have to do evil things. I sold it to Amy, not the Darkness."

"Why?"

"Because I didn't want to go to Heaven if you aren't there. I don't care about the bad stuff you've done. I love you."

"I love you too."

She made them kiss before tucking them gently back into the box. Their hands were already locked together, and nothing would ever be able to separate them.

Grork Dentist

Johanna Levene

I try to be a modern day superhero.
By day I work as a chemical engineer
building websites that encourage
the use of alternative fuels and
electric vehicles. Thursdays are the
exception, when I map transportation
systems as a Geographic Information
Science graduate student. By night, I
write stories and knit. (If I can't save
the world, I hope to at least make it
more beautiful and fuzzy.) Always, I
am a mom of wonderful Erica, wife
to pragmatic Nate, and caretaker of
our four cats and six chickens, too
numerous to name.

The pain shoots up the roots of my molar into my left eyeball as I hang up the phone. I almost cry. Through a fog, I hear a voice, "Melissa, hey, are you joining us for the deposition? Oh! You look terrible..." Kathy, my paralegal, stares down at me with concern and pats me lightly on the back. Each pat reverberates through my body like a punch in the cheek while the heavy floral scent of her perfume sets off explosions in my sinus cavities.

Cradling my face in my hand I say, "My tooth. I think I need a root canal. I mean, I've thought I needed a root canal for weeks, and I let it go too long."

A whole month until my dentist can see me. "It's August you know, and he loves his golf," his receptionist had quipped.

I expect Kathy to regale me with her own gory pus-and-blood dentist stories, but she surprises me by providing potentially useful information instead. "Oh honey, my sister lost a crown last week, and her dentist was away on some sailing vacation." I nod in empathy. "She tried that new alien dentist—are we supposed to say alien?—and raved about the experience. Let me go get Dr. Nallirk's card. My sister gave me a stack, so she could get credit for the referrals."

I consider Kathy's option. Of course, I'm aware of the Grork dentists. My worry? The potential explosive reaction when my dental phobia meets a tiny-eyed, huge-toothed, blue monster with sharp instruments. By afternoon, I'm incapacitated by pain and out of options. All the human dentists are booked into next week, and Dr. Nallirk, the Grork dentist, has an opening the next day.

The Grork's waiting room looks similar to my human dentist's waiting room but smells more like a spice store than a medical facility, with tangy notes of sweet and sharp comingling in the air. My pre-appointment stalking of Grork websites found marketing fluff explaining how the Grorks' dental philosophy is based on organic compounds from their home planet. (Nothing calms the nerves like internet research, and I wasn't sleeping through my pain anyway.) A human receptionist—her badge says *Cheryl*—checks me in and hands me a clipboard with papers to read, emphasizing, "Every page needs your initials or signature." She then offers me complimentary rallka-urk juice from a glass-fronted mini fridge.

"There are microbes in the rallka-urk juice that help to calm predental anxiety," she explains with the passion of a low-budget television commercial. It's cold, like it's come out of the freezer, and the bottle is made of a material like silicone, not glass or plastic. The avocado green liquid responds to my touch, violently effervescing where my fingers compress the container. Small particulates dance in the churning liquid. As my stomach squirms, I place the container on the desk, declining lamely, "Sorry, I don't really like fizzy drinks."

At the top of the paperwork, there are glossy handouts about "new pediatric dental implants," "total tooth replacement discounts," and "friends and family referral bonuses." One by one I initial the "not at this time" entries. By the time I get to the written description of my upcoming Grork dental procedure, all nine pages of it, the motion of looking down at my clipboard paperwork makes my tooth feel like a tiny overinflated balloon threatening to pop. I can't focus. My lawyer brain tries to send warning signals as I initial and date each page without comprehending them. When I'm done, I just sit and stare at the art on the wall: photographs that portray the ascendance of Grork dentistry over the past six years. There is the famous picture of Dr. Shalark's grand-opening of the first Grork private practice. The Manhattan skyline in the distance, Dr. Shalark is surrounded by celebrities—there is even a red carpet—and she is arm and arm with Julia Roberts. Dr. Shalark is smiling, because the lipless Grorks are always smiling, and Julia's iconic grin looks positively dainty compared to the enormous white chompers of her dentist.

A jolt from my tooth bursts my escape into reverie. Reality overcomes me. In a matter of minutes, one of these creatures is going to be my dentist. The underside of my tongue starts watering in the back of my mouth like I'm going to vomit. I try closing my eyes and breathing deeply. Just relax, I tell myself. It will all be over soon, and then you'll feel better. I open my eyes at the sound of a deep voice asking, "What do you think, Cheryl?" An attractive older man with salt-and-pepper hair smiles at the receptionist.

"Oh Greg, let me see! Did you get all six of the top fronts implanted today?" asks Cheryl.

"Nope, just four. Dr. Nallirk took out the canines to regrow. By next week, my smile will be perfect." Greg opens his mouth and shows Cheryl the gaping holes from his canine removal.

I avert my eyes and focus on the huge image of Grork arrival day directly behind Cheryl's desk; I don't want to witness this stranger's tooth sharing. I remember the Grork first-contact speech.

Sitting in the common room watching the news coverage with my college roommates, we marveled at these new beings. From the Lincoln Memorial steps—the location of all fictional and now nonfictional first contact—the cool-hued creatures promised to do us no harm and asked us to think of them as Dentists Without Borders while they grinned their huge, lipless, toothy grins. It took a couple of days for the press to get the message straight. Without lips, the Grorks can't pronounce the letter B, so the "Dentists Without Orders" message led to some panic: what, were they just globular dentists flying off the handle? It was the first of many missteps as humanity acclimated to this alien life form.

Long after my classmates returned to studying, drinking, and hooking up, I found myself returning to the empty common room for cable news Grork coverage. I'd shiver with fascination as the Grorks frankly discussed their polyamorous multisexual families. While watching perfectly coiffed news anchors try to react appropriately as Grorks discussed their decoupled physical sexual needs from their parthenogenic reproduction, I'd laugh and say out loud to the empty room, "They have sex with whoever, and don't need a partner for babies. It's not difficult to understand." Night after night the Grorks returned to news studios patiently attempting to teach away human biases.

The Grorks' earliest work was all pro-bono in underprivileged areas where the population didn't have access to dental care and legal systems didn't require licensure. The before and after pictures of kids with fractured brown teeth—bites seemingly taken out of them rather than by them—transformed into movie star smiles was powerful television. Crying mothers embracing the gummy saviors of their children turned public opinion in favor of Grork dentistry. I scan the waiting room and see the expected Pulitzer image of a decrepit school gymnasium made of concrete blocks and filled with humans in graying tattered clothes offset by Grorks in a rainbow of colors, looking like jewels performing dental miracles. As the Grork legal team leveraged positive press into Grork admission into human dental schools and eventual dental licensure, I tuned out. Aliens were fascinating; the bureaucracy of dentistry was not.

The sudden quieting of Greg and Cheryl's conversation draws my attention, and I notice them looking at me. The tooth show-off adds five bottles of rallka-urk juice to his bill. As he leaves the office, Greg shakes a bottle at me and says, "This stuff really takes the edge off!" and winks at Cheryl.

Cheryl waves at Greg, turns to me, and says, "Okay Melissa, Dr. Nallirk will see you now." I go into dental autopilot mode, gather my sheaf of signed papers, and grab my purse. I've survived root canals, gum surgery, and braces. This is just a new form of dental torture. My knees give out as I take my first step, but I use the chair to steady myself before bravely continuing to the reception desk.

Cheryl takes my paperwork, scans through the first few pages, then leads me down a hallway lined with closed, frosted glass doors. She says, "Just so you know, Dr. Nallirk identifies with he/him pronouns." Sliding open a door that looks like all the other doors, she motions me to enter, then says in a low voice, "Now, don't be nervous. I saw this is your first time visiting a Grork dentist, but it's amazing what he can do. He's replaced all my teeth with Grork implants, and I love them." She smiles and I can see Cheryl has perfect white, straight teeth, but are they a little too big? I try to investigate as I walk past her. A complaint of early Grork patients was that implant smiles were a bit too large for humans.

I settle into a normal-looking dentist chair in a room that's more spacious than a human dentist office. The doctor's stool looks like a large, clear, molded plastic nest on wheels, perfect for the Grorks' prodigious hindquarters. Although something else is different, but I can't place it until Cheryl says, "Dr. Nallirk has exceptional vision, so you won't have that bright light shining down on you during your procedure."

"It's not like this is an interrogation," says a smiling Grork bouncing into the room. From Cheryl's big smile and fake-sounding giggle, I realize they are trying to make a joke. I find the dental torture innuendo inappropriate, not funny. "Nice to see you," he pauses before mispronouncing my name, "'Ulissa." His English is a bit off and reminds me of the voice from one of those fortune teller booths: inhuman and oddly paced. He points to himself, "Dr. Nallirk," then holds out a three-fingered hand.

I reach up, expecting his hand to feel slimy, but it's more like the underbelly of a snake: cool and smooth with faint ridges. His fingers taper to sharp tips, which are extremely strong, and are used instead of dental implements during the procedure—again, from my pre-appointment research. The blue-green tinge of Dr. Nallirk's skin contrasts with the white of his lab coat. He's naked underneath, but as the Grorks' genitalia are only visible during their sexual rituals, there is no impropriety. At least, that's the social standard we humans have agreed upon with this alien race. "Nice to meet you," I belatedly respond, embarrassed that I've been staring.

"Dr. Nallirk can't pronounce the letters B, F, M, P, V or W. None of the Grorks can: no lips. That's why I use my middle name at work because my first name is Poppy," Cheryl says.

Dr. Nallirk shrugs, and his body wobbles a little, "I cannot say 'o'ee.'"

I can tell this is a practiced show. I think they want patients to understand that Dr. Nallirk's odd speech is due to physiology and not stupidity, but I can't figure out what part I'm supposed to play, so I say nothing.

After an awkward pause, Cheryl smiles. "If there is anything else you two need, I'll be in the lobby."

Dr. Nallirk plops down, scoots his chair toward me, raises my chair, and then reclines me. The throbbing in my tooth increases the lower my head gets. He evaluates me with tiny, orange eyes while his two nostril slits pulsate slowly. "So, this is your initial outing to a Grork dentist. Are you okay? Your scent is scared."

I'm in pain, feel vaguely nauseous, and the alien dentist can smell my fear, so I go with honesty. "Dr. Nallirk, I'm terrified of the dentist on the best day, and my tooth really hurts."

Dr. Nallirk throws his head back and makes a sound like a dolphin. He slaps his thigh and I watch his skin ripple up and down his torso like it's made of gelatin. "'Ulissa, thanks. I like your honesty. Let us discuss the stages. In case you get scared, just say 'halt,' and I'll halt."

After I show Dr. Nallirk which tooth hurts, he goes on to describe the procedure to fix my infected molar. He will apply Stalshirsh gel to my gums which will numb my nerves, provide an antibiotic to fight off infection, and loosen my tooth. Then he will remove the crown, exposing the tooth underneath.

He explains, "I'll add additional Stalshirsh gel and take out your tooth. Next I'll insert the Grognorg..."

I hold up my hand to stop the procedure litany, "You're just going to pull my tooth out? That's what I read online."

Dr. Nallirk says, "Stalshirsh gel loosens the tooth and quiets your hurt. It's a little scary, I know. I'll go slow, and you'll say 'halt' to any hurt."

My heart pounds and cold sweat makes my back stick to the vinyl chair. What the hell am I doing here? I'm going to let an alien put alien goop in my mouth and then rip out my tooth? The throbbing in my tooth intensifies as my face heats up and my stomach wrenches like it wants to escape from my body. I know I can't leave but each of my cells begs me to run out of this office. Shutting my eyes, I try the deep breathing trick again. Unexpectedly, I feel my heart slow and calm spreads over me. I open my eyes and see Dr. Nallirk's hands pulsating two inches above my heart in the same rhythm as his nostrils. His eyes are focused on my navel, as if he can see my insides, but then refocus to meet my gaze.

"Relaxed 'Ulissa?"

"Yes," I say, "What did you do?"

"Grork dentists use a sonar that quiets anxiety. Shall I start?"

I open my mouth in assent, and Dr. Nallirk raises his hands. They begin to shimmer as he initiates the production of anti-septic Grork fluid from glands under his skin. My desire to run has calmed, and I feel rational. I can't go home until this tooth is fixed. Dr. Nallirk dips his digits in a clay-looking pot and the gel he applies tastes like licorice and cardamom. As soon as it touches my gums, the pain recedes. I sigh.

"The tooth hurts less now, doesn't it?" Dr. Nallirk asks as he probes around my gums and mouth with his slender fingertips.

Apparently even alien dentists don't understand that patients can't talk with things in their mouths. I make a slight nod. "Great!

Let's get this old crown out." Dr. Nallirk responds. I feel a tug which shoots pain up my face, but Dr. Nallirk quickly applies more gel. As the exotic smell of Stalshirsh fills the room, my pain vanishes. Really, this isn't bad. I transport myself to an alternate reality, pretending I'm at the spa getting the newest tooth and gum facial. There is no scary clinking of metal instruments on metal trays, no chitchat with an assistant about Novocain shots, no tiny vacuum sucking my spit, and I'm not missing the whine of the drill at all. I almost enjoy the sensation of Dr. Nallirk massaging my gums to work the infection out of the tissue.

Everything is going better than I could have expected until Dr. Nallirk says, "Your tooth extraction is next." He calls out to the hallway, "Cheryl, can you get the Grognorg?" He returns his gaze back to me and says, "You should sense no hurt." I'm watching out of the corner of my eye to see what the Grognorg looks like, when I hear a sucking sound. I feel nothing but make the mistake of looking at Dr. Nallirk's hand. In two of his teal fingers is a tooth nubbin attached to a bloody root. I faint.

I wake to Cheryl and Dr. Nallirk arguing in the hallway.

"Scared 'atients need the rallka-urk juice." Dr. Nallirk says.

"I know," Cheryl replies, "And I tried, but she didn't want—"

Dr. Nallirk cuts her off. "The sonar is less good if the 'atient doesn't drink the rallka-urk." He sighs, and it's a wet sound like his disappointment is coming from deep inside his gelatinous body. "You know this, Cheryl. It's in the training.'Ulissa 'ainting is not okay. Did she sign the release 'orms? I don't need a lawsuit."

"Yes. I'm sorry. I'll do better..."

"Halt. She's alert. Go to her." Dr. Nallirk says.

Cheryl enters looking concerned. "Are you okay? Do you need me to call anyone?"

Embarrassed, I shake my head. "I'm sorry. I kind of have a hobby of fainting in the dentist's office. It always happens when I have a big appointment."

Cheryl shakes her head, "Oh, I wish you would have taken the rallka-urk juice. If you get nervous, it helps so much. Next time, you can even drink it before you come in. I'll send some home with you."

I nod, feeling ashamed that I didn't take the juice when she first offered it. A feeling not dissimilar to the shame of not flossing during a normal dentist visit.

"Dr. Nallirk will come back and explain the rest of the procedure. Are you ready?"

I nod, and Dr. Nallirk oozes in next to Cheryl and asks, "How is your tooth? Okay?"

In my embarrassment I had forgotten about my tooth. I stretch open my mouth and rub the side of my face. There is no pain and no post-root canal numbness. Other than the gap where my tooth used to be, I feel fine—no, I feel great! I smile at my new dentist. "No pain at all. Thank you so much Dr. Nallirk."

"Are you 'oozy at all?" he asks.

"No...uh...sorry about the fainting." I reply.

Dr. Nallirk keeps one hand above my heart, using his sonar to ensure I stay calm and conscious. He explains how he embedded a Grognorg into the gum cavity of my extracted tooth while I was passed out. He apologizes for not explaining the process to me earlier but said he had to do it right after the tooth was removed, or the hole would have closed. My curiosity is heightened now that I feel better. "What exactly is a Grognorg? From my research, I couldn't tell if it was a salve, an instrument, or some kind of medical device."

Dr. Nallirk looks at the clock before saying, "You are okay? I can go get another Grognorg and show you. It's the Grork secret sauce."

Cheryl's smile falters a bit as Dr. Nallirk leaves, probably afraid I'll faint again. I try to sound upbeat, "Secret sauce? He sounds almost..." I almost say human but switch to, "...American."

"I know. Sometimes I forget he's different," Cheryl says.

I marvel at how easy the procedure was. In under twenty minutes, I went from the worst pain in my life to feeling perfect. "I feel so much better. Thanks for all of your help today. How long have you worked here?"

Cheryl's full smile returns. "Almost a year now. I really like it. At first, I was nervous, but as long as you follow the Grork protocol... well the doctor is a great boss, and I believe in what he's doing: dentistry without pain."

"It really is amazing." I agree, wishing I hadn't avoided the Grork dentists for so long. "I'm sorry about not drinking the juice."

"It's okay. Next time we'll both know better." She pats my arm like I'm a newly-trained puppy.

Dr. Nallirk returns and says, "Here it is," and shows me a Grognorg floating in clear liquid near the middle of what looks like a baby food jar. It resembles a cracked egg yolk the size of a booger with a thin, red line running from its center to its edge.

Dr. Nallirk explains that the implanted Grognorg will keep the tooth cavity open while my tooth regrows in Greygnor solution. He'll make a mold from my crown to ensure the new tooth is the right shape and size. It will take about forty-eight hours to grow, then I'll be able to come back. The Grognorg in the jar pulses; it seems like it's moving closer to me. The tooth will be implanted over the Grognorg, which will first cement the tooth in place and then grow a thin film of regenerative enamel over the tooth. I think back to my late-night reading about the Grognorg. The information was vague. Dr. Nallirk says I won't ever have to worry about decay or cracks because the symbiotic Grognorg will keep my tooth healthy. By the time Dr. Nallirk's explanation is done, the little jarred, boogery Grognorg is pressing against the side of the jar closest to me, wiggling frantically.

"So the Grognorg is?" I ask, trying to reconcile this thing in the jar with something inside my mouth.

"It's a symbiotic organism from the Grork home planet," Cheryl explains with a simple candor that belies the fact that I have an alien living in my mouth. "The details were on page nine in your patient packet."

"Can I get a copy of that?" I ask, not taking my eyes from the Grognorg.

There is a long pause before Cheryl says, "Of course."

She turns to leave and I say, "Can you please take the Grognorg with you?" Dr. Nallirk hands the jar to Cheryl, the motion causing the Grognorg to float away from me.

I want to ask, "Can I eat?" and "Can I brush my teeth?" and "Did you really implant a tiny alien inside of me?" but I hide my growing anxiety by keeping my voice flat and level as I ask,

"Do I need to do anything special while I have no tooth, and the Grognorg is in place?"

"So, you should chew on a...Cheryl, how do you say it?"

Cheryl has returned with a charcoal gray, two-pocket folder. "A bone. You'll want to chew on some animal bones, unless you're a vegetarian."

Dr. Nallirk nods. "Yes, 'one. The Grognorg grows stronger eating 'one. You can chew eggshells too."

"These instructions will explain everything," Cheryl says as she pulls out a trifold pamphlet printed on thick, creamy paper featuring the image of a beautiful, smiling woman who doesn't fear dentists or aliens. Later she will smudge and wrinkle from my sweaty hands as I read and reread the information. Already I am worrying. Could the Grognorg dissolve my jaw bone?

"I've also included the business card of Throck, our Grork legal counsel, in case you need any additional information about the paperwork you were provided." Cheryl points to a turquoise business card trapped in the folder's pocket-triangles.

My mind spins, but I paste on a big smile to convince Dr. Nallirk and Cheryl things are fine. I obediently make an appointment for my tooth implantation, pay my copay, and take a stack of Dr. Nallirk's business cards for my friends along with a postcard asking again if I want more information on total replacement or payment programs. Throughout the transaction, my tongue is a timid explorer, darting in and out of the space between my teeth. I'm not remembering any information on Grognorg removal in my pre-appointment paperwork, but I'll be looking closely when I get back to the office. Cheryl presses a cold bottle of rallka-urk juice into my sweaty hand and urges me to drink it before the next appointment. "It will help with the anxiety, and it really tastes great," she says. Dr. Nallirk nods in agreement, putting his three-fingered hand on Cheryl's shoulder and grinning his perpetual smile.

Waiting for the elevator, I pull out the stapled release form while balancing the bottle of turbulent juice. My pain long forgotten, I now scan with a practiced eye. All the information is here in obfuscating legal and dental mumbo jumbo. As I ride down to the ground floor, I find details on the rallka-urk juice, the tooth extraction, the sonar, the alien Grognorg, and its bone fetish hidden in a small font glossary on page nine. Everything questionable or scary is in the back, basically ensuring patients will never read it. It's not illegal, but providing pages of marketing materials first then hiding important information in an appendix is worth a review by our firm's malpractice attorney. A single colorful postcard tumbles to the floor, and I scoop it up. I read and process the information about the new Grork pediatric dentistry offering. Has anyone considered what long-term exposure to Grognorgs will do to human children?

Outside in the parking lot, my hands tremble as I throw the bottle of rallka-urk juice in a trash can. I have enough aliens in my body, thank you very much. The container makes a wet farting sound as it hits the bottom of the bagless can and juice leaks onto the sidewalk. Belatedly, I wonder what will happen if the alien microbes enter the storm water system. In my car, I turn the rearview mirror and watch my tongue slide into the empty cavity between my teeth, pretending I cannot feel the slimy, pulsing Grognorg hungering for bone.

Vincent Coriolis, Father of the Nation

Celia Neri

Celia Neri was born in 1978 on the shores of the Mediterranean Sea in a multicultural family. She studied Comparative Literature in Paris before coming back to Southern France where she now lives.

A lifelong science-fiction and fantasy reader, she realised in early 2017 she also had stories to tell and started creative writing, often with an emphasis on characters who reflect aspects of her own identity.

As usual, they all press against me, and the first question always is, "Why didn't you go into government afterwards?" I give them the answer I always give: that I had a daughter I wanted to go back to, that I was no stateswoman anyway, that Vincent Coriolis was the right man for the job. They nod, smiling. What I'm telling them is what they are expecting, what they want to hear: the faithful sidekick went back to being a good mother while the hero of the Revolution started the reforms that changed the colony and galactic commerce; he became the Father of the Nation, I returned to my disabled child.

It's all a lie, obviously. But what would be the point of telling them the truth when they so eagerly believe the legend?

I go to my bike and encourage them to do the same. "The tour is going to start soon, ladies, persons and gentlemen! Please check your bike, that your headset works for sending and receiving, and don't forget to wear your high visibility vest."

The ten tourists prepare themselves with empty chatter and laughter. I sigh inwardly. Fifteen years ago, I gave orders to the troops storming Parliament. These days, I shepherd bikers through the notable monuments of Gorne. Marina Herikis, former right-hand woman of Vincent Coriolis, tourist guide.

At the centre of the Revolution Plaza stands a three foot tall statue of Vincent; he gazes to the stars, his arm extended in a gesture of friendship to the other mining colonies. A couple of tourists glance its way, surprised I don't start by a grovelling allocution that would celebrate his tireless work to reestablish unions—an ancient Earth custom that had disappeared—or to offer subsidized health services to the elderly. Instead, we turn our back to it, pedalling into the warren of small streets that surround the Revolution Plaza.

I begin my speech which is relayed to their headsets.

"We are now in Half-Hanged-Man Street. The buildings in here date back to the first year of the colonisation, all timber and stone, close to one another to defend against the planetoid original predators. No one ever redeveloped the area which is why there are no boulevards, no avenues, no places into which a glider can venture. Pedestrians and bikers only. These narrow streets were incredibly useful during the Revolution. We could easily put up defences and block the way. From the safety of the barricade, we shot at any Loyalist troop coming at us."

We turn the corner of Half-Hanged-Man Street. This is where Leola fell on the last night.

It had seemed at first like such an ordinary night during the Revolution.

I was checking on the old town defences; Vincent was gathering the troops at the West Corner market to take down a rocket launcher in the morning early hours. A couple of Loyalist soldiers had made a half-hearted attempt to come at us at the entrance of the street, we had repelled them. Later, Leola had decided it was as good a time as any to go and check on her elderly grandmother, only to find two soldiers who were trying to sneak on us from behind.

"How was it?" asks a tourist through the mike of his headset. "How did it feel to be at the heart of the action?"

There's always one who asks that. Usually, they're into their early fifties, like me. They were old enough to have taken part in the revolution but never did. It doesn't prevent them basking in the glory of it and lap up any epic crap I tell them.

"Often frightening. But we were resolute."

We had pissed ourselves when we realised two soldiers had snuck behind us and killed Leola. It was the shots ringing that alerted us. A fair few numbers of weapons, both on our side and on the Loyalist side, were still old bullet and powder rifles, not the fancy new ray guns.

We left a couple of us to hold the barricade and I led a dozen revolutionaries down the dark street, towards the sound of the shooting. No one wanted to go but we needed to. It was either that or be killed one by one. There was Flower, Rahma, Ekfrasis, Gayn, Barrin, Stuphras, and so many others whose names and faces I have now forgotten. Gayn was playing brave, walking right behind me, but I could hear his teeth chattering.

We found Leola's corpse, her blood mingling with that of a soldier she had managed to shoot before falling. He wasn't dead yet. I looked at him with disgust. We now had the unsavoury task of trying to make him talk. We needed to know where the other one was, how they had managed to arrive here. He was unlikely to provide the information gracefully.

We emerge from the old town warren.

"We are arriving onto Lapsichord Plaza, ladies, persons and gentlemen, where we will have our first stop."

I lead the bikers to the centre of the plaza, zig-zagging to avoid other bikers and pedestrians. The statue of a bronze roaring lion stands proudly, surrounded by a gaggle of tourists snapping pics of it with their comms. We stop a few paces from it and dismount.

They all start drinking, wiping sweat from their brows. A couple take out hats and sunglasses from their saddlebags. I wait until they have gathered around me to start again.

"Lapsichord Plaza played an important part during the Revolution. Unbeknownst to us, there was a secret entrance by the statue side that led to an underground chamber where Loyalists and the former government had hidden weapons and provisions. This cache was instrumental in them holding out for so long in the Eastern Quarter, since Lapsichord Plaza is located at the entrance of it."

"When did you realise it?" asks a tourist.

"It was actually on the very last night of the Revolution."

"Was it Vincent Coriolis who led the attack?" asks another.

"For goodness sake, where is Vincent?" Gayn was muttering.

We were huddled in the shadow of the bronze lion. I still couldn't believe our luck that we had managed to cross the plaza without cover unspotted. The dying soldier had told us where his colleague was heading to and we had followed him at a distance. We had all stood shocked when we had seen him opening a door cleverly concealed in the plinth decorations.

"Flower left barely half an hour ago. Give them time." I replied in a barely audible voice.

The confidence in my voice was fake. I wasn't wondering where Vincent was; I was wondering if he would come. Since our movement had swept the colony and we had arrived at the capital, carried by a wave of revolutionary frenzy, he had become more and more distant. In turn, I had sought duties that took me away from his side. He had cronies enough around him anyway. But what put me most ill-at-ease were those moments when we saw each other. He avoided my glance. I had never been one of these *pasionarias* we had met, women eager to lay down their lives for the Revolution. I just had stuff to do to make the world right, and I did it, however repulsive I found it. I was only hoping for some support from the man I stood up with when it all first started in a tiny village on the Eastern Marches, when we had both almost been executed for resisting the company's taxes, saved by a mob as angry as we were.

He was slippery like an eel nowadays.

Half an hour later, Flower still hadn't come back. No sign of Vincent or of any support.

"Damn it," I cursed. "We're going in. We have the element of surprise."

The group is marvelling at the historical artefacts in the subterranean vaulted chamber. It has become a tourist attraction and it recreates the place as I had found it twenty years ago. Crates of weapons piled upon themselves, rolled blankets in which soldiers caught a quick nap. Wax statues represented Loyalists playing cards in faithfully recreated uniforms.

I stand at the exact same spot I stood all these nights ago and go on with my speech.

"The attack was quick and successful."

The shots rang out as we made our way down the stairs.

"We only had one casualty."

I saw Rahma stumbling down, her beautiful dark hair forming a halo before her body hit the ground dully.

"When we had overpowered the soldiers, we discovered all that you are seeing now: the weapons, the food the government was using to buy loyalty. We sent one of us back to the barricade at Half-Hanged-Man Street so that we could seize it all."

Little Barrin went. Barely sixteen. He made it safely there, warned them all. He was overjoyed and did a victory dance on the barricade. A passing Loyalist soldier took a pot shot from half a mile away with a ray gun he had been issued with and hit him in the head.

"This is when we heard for the first time of the conspiracy going on; the one that would precipitate the events. What you have to realise is that we never planned for the Revolution to end that night. We were in for the long haul, to fight skirmishes, to convince people to let go of the status quo. But what we learned here and then changed the course of events."

The soldier was sniggering, slumped against the wall, a bubble of blood and spit forming at his lips, inflating with each of his chuckles.

"Why are you laughing?" I asked him angrily.

"Because I recognise you. You're Coriolis' sidekick aren't you? The woman who couldn't pay her taxes because of her disabled daughter and who stood up with him?"

"What if I am?"

"Where's your hero tonight, O faithful companion?"

A cold sweat broke on my back and made me shiver. Flower hadn't come back. Had anything happened...?

"Well, I'll tell you. For free."

He sniggered some more.

"Since I'm about to die, anyway...He's at the palace."

"We learned that this very night, barely an hour ago, Vincent Coriolis had been captured as he was making his way towards the Western Market. He had been brought to the palace, most probably to be executed the following morning."

The tourists around me gasp. It's history now, they all know how it ends, that Vincent survives, that he becomes a hero of the Revolution, the new President, the Great Reformer, Father of the Nation. But it's always so satisfying for my ego to hear them gasp because they are taken by my tale.

"The captured soldier revealed to us that Vincent had been betrayed by a newly recruited revolutionary. The company and its puppet government were now planning to use him as an example to quell the Revolution."

Such a perfect lie I recite too.

"Who captured him?"

I was frantic. I had kneeled down next to the soldier and grabbed him by his lapel. I may have grown apart from Vincent, but he was the figurehead of the Revolution, the dashing man who fought our oppressors, the person who held together warring factions towards a common goal. His death would have meant the end of all our efforts.

All my fellow revolutionaries are tensed around me. I know the same thoughts are crossing their minds, to say nothing of their worry that someone they admire so much, love even, could die.

"Captured?" said the soldier. "Who said anything about capture? He's very cosy with President Karn, you know. Has been for weeks now."

"Liar!" screamed Gayn.

Before I could prevent it, he had shot the soldier in the head. His body slumped further in my grip and I released it.

I looked around us. It was a scene of carnage. There were dead soldiers everywhere, and Rahma lying on the cold ground. On the faces of my companions, I saw no elation that we had taken such a strategic place, only worry, anger and confusion.

I sat down. I felt strangely detached from it all. Maybe it was shock. Maybe my brain was just reevaluating everything I had witnessed these past few weeks, and this reveal perfectly made sense in the context. Vincent watering down his speeches and saying afterwards that it was to better convince the people sitting on the fence; Vincent changing quarters despite the fact he was hidden at a most loyal household; Vincent asking me about my daughter though he had never given a care after that first day when we had risen together.

My companions had overcome their shock and were urging me to go to the palace. That it was all a ploy, obviously. That we had to save Vincent.

I gingerly rose to my feet. Such brave men and women didn't deserve leaders like Vincent or me.

"We immediately decided to attack the palace. It was just a few of us. We had no time to look for support and it would have been dangerous anyway, with Loyalists hidden at every street corner."

We are back on the bikes and pedalling under the summer sun. Gorne streets are lively with joyful passers-by, brightly painted shops, restaurants advertising the best fare in the city. A sight so at odds with the night I'm recounting. I know the tourists are both morbidly fascinated by my tale and enjoying what surrounds us, a place so full of life, proclaiming so loudly "We have a happy ending for you at the end of the journey!" No one asks me questions anymore. They all seem seized by the same urgency we had that night, moving swiftly towards the palace, towards the dénouement.

"And here we are, ladies, persons and gentlemen! The palace back door!"

Someone chuckles and I understand why. The words "back door" have hardly ever been used for a three meters tall gate, made of black decorated strong wood, and reinforced by steel bands. It is a remnant of the past, when the mining colony was first established and people defended themselves with what was at hand.

I point to a small door at the side of it. People always overlook it.

"Obviously, we weren't going to attack the back door, there weren't enough of us. We needed a quiet entrance. The actual back door was to be it."

I lead the tourists to the small entrance which stands open and smile to the guard. I recognise him. I come often enough that he recognises me too.

"Borek!" I whispered at the closed door while quietly rasping it. "For goodness sake, Borek! Open this damn door! I know you're here, I checked your rota yesterday!"

He wasn't happy to see us. We had planted him at the palace guards months ago, on manning duties, in the hope he would be useful. I suspected he had become used to receiving a salary and a solid meal three times a day. It was much better than his previous employment in the uranium mines in the Southern hemisphere where people died every day.

They all began climbing the dark narrow steps in a single line. I remained behind with Borek who was frowning in the half light of a torch.

"I wasn't expecting you..." he started saying.

He never had time to finish his complaint. I put a hand on his mouth, slid a knife in his belly and pulled it up to the heart. I felt sick as I saw his body crumpling to the floor. I didn't know if he would have betrayed us or not. I didn't know if he knew Vincent was in the palace and if he would have warned him or anyone else. I still don't. But I couldn't take any chances.

I hurried to join the others, glad no one could see my face in the barely lit stairs. Tears were streaming freely and my stomach was heaving. It took me the five minutes needed to reach the landing closed by a door to finally get a grip on myself.

"This is it, ladies, persons and gentlemen! The president's office! Right across the landing at the top of this little known staircase."

Some of the tourists were panting because of the steep climb. Others were looking around them. The office was a vast room, lavishly decorated with golden cornices, tapestries and old oil paintings. Deep rugs were covering the floor and plush armchairs and sofas were scattered here and there. A huge desk dominated the room.

"Of course, you are all wondering how come such a potential

safety issue could ever happen. A secret staircase leading almost directly from the street to the President's office and the door guarded by a single man?"

One of the tourists raises a hand. "I heard it was built when the first CEO of the company led the colony, because he enjoyed..." She blushes before going on, "Prostitutes."

"It's exactly right. And President Karn was using it for the exact same purposes, and I suppose many others before him."

The tourists frown and tut. Such deplorable morals, we are so well rid of this lot, they all thinking, I'm sure.

"But before we could arrive into this office, we had to fight the people guarding its door."

Happily, no one ever asks why we headed to the President's office rather than going to the prison cells where Vincent should have been kept. Maybe they think that Karn was a villain not too dissimilar from those you see in vids, twirling his moustache as he gloated to the hero about his nefarious plans.

Gayn and Ekfrasis had burst from the staircase and silently dispatched the two guards with their knives before they could even raise the alarm.

"You go," Gayn told me. "We hold the corridor."

They took positions: Ekfrasis at the corner; Gayn in front of the door; Stuphras at the other end; Mechil, Asin, Rold, all standing alert, their rifles ready. My last glimpse was of Runa tying her hair back in a ponytail so it wouldn't hinder her.

I opened the door.

Vincent hastily rose from the armchair he was comfortably

sitting in. Surprised, but composed. I barely glanced at Karn who was behind his desk.

"Were they torturing him?" asks a tourist.

Vincent put down the cigar he was smoking and the glass of cognac he was drinking.

"I didn't expect you," he said coolly.

"I didn't expect to find you here," I replied as coolly.

He shrugged.

I think that's what annoyed me most. He shrugged, as if it was a mild inconvenience that I found him cosy with Karn, a normal development not even worth mentioning.

"I can tell you Vincent was fighting like a lion in this office," I say to the tourists who are listening to me with bated breath.

"So it was all...What?" I said angrily. "A scam? A sham? A con? Get the peasants to fight for you until you get to the riches?"

He lifted hands to placate me. It didn't. It incensed me.

"Calm down. I believed every single word I said. I do think our capitalist system is in its last throes. We need to get rid of it. Taxes benefit the shareholders, poor people need three jobs to survive. It can't go on. But maybe we should go for it gradually. Before you barged in, I was right in the middle of delicate negotiations, you know."

I saw red. I caught him, hand in the safe, happily taking from the same pot of gold everyone had been taking from for two centuries, and still he lied, pretending, just like the others, he was doing it for the greater good.

The unmistakable sound of rifle shooting erupted from behind the door. People were fighting in the corridor. They were fighting for a colony that would be more just, against a system that didn't make sense anymore considering technology and the current galactic situation. They were dying for a man they believed in.

I took a quick pace towards the desk, and in one swift movement, I pulled my gun and shot President Karn.

I turned again towards Vincent.

"Congratulations," I said coldly. "You have now won the Revolution."

"...And then Vincent shot President Karn!"

The tourists gasp again and erupt in cheers and applause.

When they have calmed down, one asks, "How did it go right after?"

"Vincent went to the corridor, telling the soldiers to stand down, that they had lost."

All dead, all dead lying on the cold marble floor. Gayn and Ekfrasis and Stuphras and Mechil, Asin and Rold, and Runa with her ponytail.

"He then started immediately the important reforms which have changed our planetoid and commerce. The idea we would get rid of capitalism was obviously nothing more than that: an ideal, a youthful fancy. It didn't stand to scrutiny in the face of reality. But we are now living in a fairer, more just place, thanks to him and to the men, women and persons who fought in the Revolution. He turned a colony into a nation that showed the way to the entire galaxy."

They break into applause again. I know there are no gods because I have never been hit by lightning while I tell such barefaced lies.

We leisurely make our way back from the palace to the Revolution plaza where we took the bikes.

When it's time to part, I find them all again surrounding me. They have trouble letting go of the golden tale I spun them.

"Do you still see Vincent?" asks one.

"His schedule is very busy but, from time to time, we send each other messages via our comms," I reply with a gentle smile. They all beam back. They probably think I send him words of encouragement and that he enquires about my health and family. My last actual message to him, a year ago, was, "You should have been hanged with Karn's Loyalists, you arsehole!" to which he had replied, "Go back to changing your daughter's nappies and driving tourists around town, rabid woman!"

Eventually, they all shake my hand in turn.

"It was so educational, thank you."

"I had a wonderful day. It made me proud of my nation."

"Thank you so much for sharing your experiences. It was inspirational."

"I felt like I became part of history thanks to you."

And so on, and so forth. Finally, they're all gone. They've probably already forgotten my name. It's just as good.

Night has fallen and the orange glow of the sodium lamps illuminate the streets. I tie my bike to the wall and shoulder my bag again. I feel sore from the all the pedalling. I should try finding another job before my body decides it's too old for this or before I'm fired. How would I pay the bills then? I awkwardly make my way towards the tube to go back home and hope the tips the tourists gave me will be enough to buy food.

We won. Yay.

Into Nothingness

T.D. Walker

T.D. Walker is the author of Small
Waiting Objects (CW Books, 2019),
a collection of her science fiction
poetry. Her poems and stories have
appeared in Strange Horizons,
Web Conjunctions, The Cascadia
Subduction Zone, The Future Fire,
and elsewhere. Find out more at her
website: https://www.tdwalker.net.

1.

In her human body, Madison sits.

In her new, alien body, Mia dances.

Mia had always lived in her human body in ways that Madison couldn't: she'd run marathons, she'd eaten grasshoppers and snakes, and she never had half-finished Chardonnay bottles clanking in her fridge door. And the men. And the stories she'd told. All while Madison sat and watched.

Madison, Mia's twin. *Fraternal* twin.

And here in her new, alien body, Mia dances.

Another guest arrives. Goodbye, 2038. Hello, 2039.

Really, Mia shouldn't be here. Not in this form. Not that anyone who knew her before the transformation would see anything different. Madison wasn't quite sure how Mia had left the facility, only that she had knocked on Madison's apartment door dressed for the party. "It's New Year's Eve," Mia said. "Get dressed."

So she dressed.

Madison hadn't expected her sister's new body to be so

expressive. Not after wrapping Nick's car around the tree, not after the burns. For days, Mia lay so still in the hospital bed at the facility, the morphine drip keeping her from screaming and thrashing as she'd done in the ER. As she'd done when the doctors told her about Nick. As she'd done when she'd seen herself, all burns and no skin. As she'd done when they'd backed her off the morphine. Mia needed a clear head when she pushed the button to start the process that allowed her to become this.

Not dead. The techs at the facility never used the word "dead." Is there a word for this kind of death in the aliens' language? Their language, their technology, their request to meet humans who'd seen earth first-hand, who knew it intimately.

Of course, they wouldn't want the dead, dead.

Not after coming all that way. Which is what Uncle Oliver had told them. It was his company that had found the alien's probe around the asteroid. Her parents had met K. Oliver Hall back before Bayou City Oil and Mining International had even proposed mining whatever it was they mined out there. Uncle Oliver told them that what the aliens wanted was simple. Human minds in indestructible bodies. Humans to visit them. Not the dead, the living. The vital. Mia, vital and alive.

Mia had a funeral though. A private ceremony. Could she feel her brain being liquefied? Madison didn't want to ask. She didn't want to ask Mia if she had seen her old body after her brain had been recreated in the newly-generated one. She did know that Mia wanted her earthly remains buried next to her husband's, who will trade his broken human body for a new artificial one tomorrow.

The obituary—or the news of the transformation—will come later, after Bayou City Oil announces the launch of the transformed out to the asteroid where they'll board the alien ship. Uncle Oliver had taken care of whatever needed to be done to get Nick and Mia from the public ER to the privacy of the facility before anyone found out about it.

Uncle Oliver had always taken care of whatever needed to be done for Mia.

Mia. Will anyone here know that they celebrated the dying year with a dead woman? Madison will. And Owen.

Goodbye, 2038. Hello, 2039. Across the room, Mia dances with Owen. Someone had pointed him out to her at Mia and Nick's wedding weeks ago as the one who'd started the pools: who'd wind up taking home the bouquet, the garter, the awkward bridesmaid. Madison knew that must have been her. She hadn't known most of the wedding guests, and she doesn't know most of the guests here at this iteration of Nick and Owen's infamous New Year's Eve parties. These are Nick's friends, coworkers, poker buddies. Were.

Next week, Nick will be dead, Mia will still be dead, and their new bodies will be hurtling into nothingness. Madison pats the gray-muzzled dog that pushes its way into the chair with her. She opens one of the champagne bottles. Too much champagne for the people here. More like a wake than a New Year's Eve party.

Across the room, Mia laughs. Madison pours herself another flute of champagne. Cheap, too sweet. She already spilled a bit on her dress, the same black dress she'd worn to the funeral. Long lacy sleeves, pleated skirt. "That thing?" Mia said both times when she saw what Madison wore. Madison's ex had thought it had a vintage charm. Her ex, who's dancing with someone else across town now.

Dancing, laughing. Madison looks up. One of the strangers is looking at her. Probably pitying her. He looks away, then back at Mia. Not pity for her? Or pity for her for having the dead sister who pretends to be alive? Mia is worse than a ghost. People don't believe in ghosts—there isn't anything there when you look closely in the light. But when you look closely at her, Mia, this Mia, remains.

Goodbye, 2038. Hello, 2039.

Tomorrow, Madison will help Mia sort through her things in the apartment she shared for a few weeks with Nick. They'll go through his things, too. Then Mia and Nick will be off, together. Outer space. And that will be that. This is the pitiable thing: that Mia died, that she came back and can pretend to be Mia for a while before she's gone again. A second death.

Madison empties the flute and refills it. Mia will ask Madison what she wants from her things: dresses, jewelry, the exquisite small *objets* you get when you get married. Madison will ask for her running shoes instead. She won't be able to ask for the one thing she wants, which is for her sister to stay on, haunting her, keeping her from letting herself slip more and more towards nothingness.

2.

Mia should sit with Madison, getting drunk on Nick's champagne, but she is here, warm, dancing. Dancing. Using the dance lessons Nick surprised her with for their wedding, though she'd learned the steps years before. The movements came back to her at the lessons. Movement always comes back to her, even now, even in this body. Mia and Nick danced once after classes, at their reception; they planned on making nights of it later. Except.

The strangest part about her new body so far is that she can't remember having the burns on her old one. She remembers headaches, hangovers, the time she fell from that window, even if she can't feel the pain. She wonders if this is what Nick feels, trapped inside his body, his spinal cord no longer talking to that complicated brain of his. "Are you in pain?" she asked him after she got her new body and went to see him. He blinked twice quickly: no. "I'm not either," she said. "Not now, anyway."

If she admits to herself that she can't remember the accident, that would be stranger still.

Uncle Ollie said not to worry about it. She won't worry about it.

She shouldn't be here. She decides not to worry about that, either.

Mia held Nick's hand in the facility. She imagined that it would be the reverse of what she actually felt: her hand, so warm, so lifelike, holding his toneless hand in hers. No response from his, as if this part of him were dead already.

No, they aren't dead. Nick wants to stay in his body until the morning after the year changes. Something about finishing out the year, which had been, up until the accident, one of the best of his life, he said on their wedding day. Mia wanted out as soon as she could. Hard for him to say more than yes or no without the optical scanner and the alphabet screen thingy, though. Mia was never patient enough for anything but yes or no even before all this.

They will give Nick a device he can operate with his eyes—he'll have to look at a series of shapes in a certain pattern to get the process started. They gave Mia a button, which she smashed with her fist. Then she woke up in her new body. Then she realized that she smelled of gravel and metal, something plastic and new.

"You're okay with me going tonight?" Three quick blinks: yes. She kissed him.

Yes, he said it. Maybe Nick didn't want her to go, still doesn't. And Owen. Uncle Ollie could fix that. Who here would believe it about the aliens, anyway? Nick would tell her that she's careless, going to the party. But how were they going to argue about it? They argue too much. No more, Mia decides. They argued about the party days before the accident. Mia didn't want to invite Madison, who'd mope, but Nick said her sister should be sad about her ex dumping her just before Nick and Mia's wedding. Mia didn't want to invite Owen, but Nick pointed out that he and Owen were throwing the party at the house he and Owen used to share, so that was that. He and Owen. Her Nick. So Mia would suffer Madison and Owen sulking as their friends drank themselves out of 2038.

Suffer—what a strange word. She can't remember the accident. That, along with whatever happened after she pushed the button, is thankfully gone from her mind. She won't ask Nick about it. She knows they argued about something—this?—and that they were driving. Who was driving? Then she woke up in the hospital, hearing herself scream before she knew why she was screaming.

She should sit with Madison. The guy Owen said he'd invite to introduce to Madison will be here soon. Ted? Tom? She hadn't told Madison about him. Just in case. Just in case she needed to prove to herself that this new body was as capable as her old one had been.

She should sit with Madison, but here she is, doing this awkward cha-cha with Owen. He's too tall. She presses her face—her new familiar face—into his chest. He smells like whiskey, like barbecue, like aftershave. Nick's brand. He smells so human after the hospital. Tomorrow, she'll be in the hospital again, waiting for Nick to wake up in his new body. The day after, she'll be aboard a ship hurtling away from earth.

Human, but only just. This will be her last night among people, just as a person. She feels Owen drawing her closer. He won't kiss her. Not in front of everyone. But there's midnight. That excuse.

She will kiss him. Two hours before midnight. Keep dancing. Then she'll tilt her head up and kiss him. Owen knows Nick in a way that no one else but Mia does—she wants her new body to know old Nick the same way. Mia will kiss Owen, kiss his memories of Nick as he was, kiss his memories of who Nick was when he and Owen shared the house, the way Owen watched Mia and Nick kissing in the almost-darkness of the hallway.

She will kiss him before they all have to die once again.

3.

One of them is Nick's late wife. The other one is her surviving sister.

Tim settles onto a bar stool and starts on the bottle of whiskey. Not traditional for New Year's Eve, but it's what he managed to lift from his ex-father-in-law's unlocked wet bar last time he was there to pick up the kids. It's vile. Not that his ex-father-in-law would leave the good stuff out, but this is worse than usual. Not his doing then. His ex-wife's. He raises his glass to his ex-wife and swallows the shot while trying not to taste it. He looks at the one in the chair.

He tries to get Owen's attention, but Owen only sees the one he's dancing with. Tim wasn't sure why Owen had been so insistent that he come. But there was so much Tim wasn't sure of. He wasn't sure why he'd been invited to join Owen's weekly poker game. He wasn't sure why Owen had let him go on about his ex-wife as long as he had after their last game.

And he wasn't sure why he believed what Owen said about Nick. Sure, Nick had been in an accident. But the aliens? And the new body? Something about the way Owen said what he'd said made Tim feel certain that Nick and his wife were in a secret facility somewhere, getting body-swapped with alien technology so that they could go into outer space. Owen had made Tim swear not to tell anyone else. Owen wasn't supposed to tell anyone. But Owen had told him.

The one sitting and the one dancing must be the sisters. Not a strong resemblance. Just that unmistakable judging smirk siblings reserve for one another. The one in the chair aims it at the dancing one.

The sitting one must be the dead one, jealous of the living one dancing. Perhaps her new body isn't capable of dancing? Alien technology, who knows.

Owen told him that the dead one and Nick will sail off into space together, happily ever after, in their alien bodies with their minds intact. Tim drinks his whiskey. Nick is young, his wife had been young before she changed bodies. When Tim and his ex had first married, he'd have signed up to spend eternity with her. It wouldn't have taken long, though, for him to see his mistake. Is this why the dead one is so sad in her chair? Regret is a strange thing.

But then there's the living one. Dancing. Laughing.

Surely, the dead one can still do that. There's a loveliness about her, the dead one, sitting in her chair. All emotion, like some bronze of a woman caught in the moment of—what is that expression? Tim wants her. Tim wants to ask her to dance. Tim wants to ask her what it's like to die and to come back and was she always this beautiful? The dead one can't dance—she'd be dancing otherwise, right? And she'll go off with Nick soon. And the whiskey, his ex's vile whiskey, is making him confident and sick.

A half-hour before midnight, Tim leaves the almost-empty bottle on the bar. Owen hasn't looked away from the dancing one. Tim mumbles his thanks to Owen from across the room, grabs his coat, and heads toward the door. Before he opens it, he stops and looks at the dead one again. He watches her hand stroking Owen's old dog, her hand so alive, so sensitive. He can't change that he'd let another year slip by, that it will be 2039 tomorrow. Nothing to be done about that. And nothing to be done about the fact that soon, the dead one will be gone, floating out there into nothingness, and he'll never see her again.

4.

Because Mia asks him to dance with her.

Because Mia presses herself—her new artificial body—against his while they are dancing.

Because Nick isn't here. Because Nick can't be here.

Because human Nick will die tomorrow and artificial Nick with human Nick's mind will go to meet the aliens. Because he'll be going with Mia.

Because he took to calling her The Hungry One after Nick announced over carbo-loading with her at their house—Nick and Owen's—the night before Nick's first marathon that he'd be moving in with her. Because she took the last of the linguine with clams after Owen had raised a toast to them. Because

Owen can't remember Nick running errands much less marathons before Mia claimed him.

Because Mia must be hungry again.

Because Owen took to calling her "boyish" to tease Nick. Because Nick asked him to stop. Because she is boyish and sporty and compact and hungry. Because she is beautiful.

Because Nick hadn't really left Owen for Mia.

Because Owen never committed to Nick. Because Owen never admitted to himself or anyone else that those afternoons holding Nick while they looked out over the lake behind their house made him wonder if this is what his—Owen's—marriage should have been like. Because Owen had been married to his college sweetheart. Because Owen and his husband grew up and apart and angry at each other for doing so.

Because if Mia, the human Mia, died, then she and Nick are no longer married.

Because the human Mia is dead.

Because Owen had been divorced for five years now.

Because he and Nick never were. Because Owen couldn't take that risk again.

Because in the hospital, when he asked Nick if he'd miss him, the nurse laughed. Because she asked Owen why Nick would miss him when he'd get to see all those stars and the aliens and this wonderful afterlife after the pain and the paralysis and the closeness of death. Because Nick blinked three times in reply.

Because Owen couldn't remember if three blinks meant yes or no.

Because next week, Nick and Mia will be gone. Because that will be their nothingness to face, not his.

Because Owen will be here alone in the house, looking at the lake, the moon blinking twice, three times at him when the wind catches the water. Because this will be his nothingness to face alone.

Because Owen knows this look, Mia's hunger. Because it might be for him—for Owen—or for what she knows he and Nick had shared. Because he isn't sure. Because she interrupted it.

Because Mia's hunger is aimed at him.

Because if he says yes, it will be an intractable, horrible "yes" to the world.

Because she looks up at him.

Because the music pauses for the countdown to midnight. Because they all stop drinking and dancing and laughing and patting the dog who likes Nick more than he ever liked Owen. Because they all stop.

Because he doesn't know whose world he'll say "yes" to.

THANK YOU TO OUR SUPPORTERS

Many thanks to our patrons and supporters, especially:

**Stephanie Johnston • Cathrin Hagey
S Naomi Scott • Natalie Weizenbaum
Siobhan Beeman**

**Emily Anderson • Felicia OSullivan • J'nae Spano
Katherine Montalto • Kennon Hulett
Martin Cohen • Salomao Becker
Shannon White • Tamara Rutledge • Tory Hoke
Bonnie Warford • Kara • Frederick Stark**

**Carly Racklin • Charlotte Nash-Stewart
GriffinFire • Isabel Cañas • Jen G • Jocelyn Actual
Karen Anderson • Kayla • Liz Warner
Maria Haskins • Suzanne Thackston**

Want to see your name here? Become a patron!
patreon.com/lunastation

 patreon

About the Cover Artist

Caitlyn illustrates the fantastic & fanciful, the historic & strange. She is most often found wandering around many of the grand gardens & museums of Los Angeles, CA.

You can find more of her work at:

caitlynkurilich.com

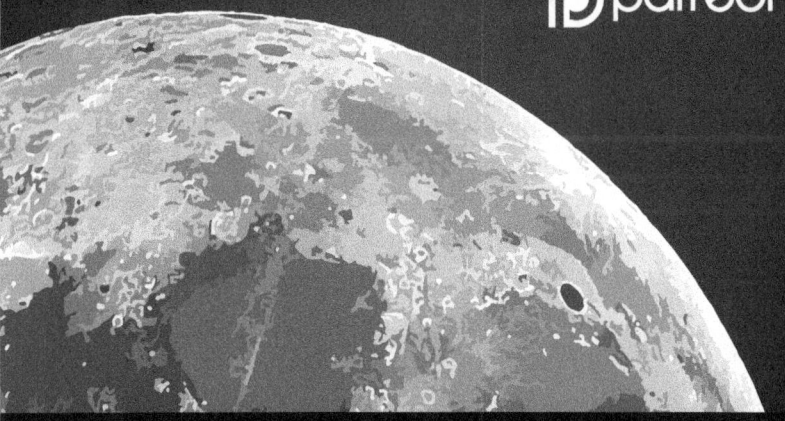